I0523035

THE MOLE TRAIN

ALSO BY JOHN REED

Van Gogh's Gypsy
Dark Forest
Thirteen Mountain
Shadow White as Stone
The Kingfisher's Call
Assume the Position
Mountain of Ashes

THE MOLE TRAIN

A LABYRINTH OF SOULS NOVEL

BY

JOHN REED

ShadowSpinners Press

Copyright © 2020 John Reed

All rights reserved,
including the right to reproduce this book,
or portions thereof, in any form.

Cover art by Josephe Vandel.
Book design by Matthew Lowes.

ShadowSpinners Press
shadowspinnerspress.com

Typeset in
Minion Pro by Robert Slimbach
and IM FELL Double Pica by Igino Marini.
The Fell Types are digitally reproduced
by Igino Marini, www.iginomarini.com.

Learn more about
the Labyrinth of Souls game at
matthewlowes.com/games.

To Jodi who gave me faith—and a great title.

Editor's Preface

Dungeon Solitaire: Labyrinth of Souls is a fantasy game for tarot cards, written by Matthew Lowes and Illustrated by Josephe Vandel. In the game you defeat monsters, disarm traps, open doors, and explore mazes as you delve the depths of a dangerous dungeon. Along the way you collect treasure and magic items, gain skills, and gather companions.

Now ShadowSpinners Press is publishing this and other stand-alone novels inspired by the game. Each *Labyrinth of Souls* novel features a journey into a unique vision of the underworld.

The Labyrinth of Souls is more than an ancient ruin filled with monsters, trapped treasure, and the lost tombs of bygone kings. It is a manifestation of a mythic underworld, existing at a crossroads between people and cultures, between time and space, between the physical world and the deepest reaches of the psyche. It is a dark mirror held up to human experience, in which you may find your dreams … or your doom. Entrances to this realm can appear in any time period, in any location. There are innumerable reasons why a person may enter, but it is a place antagonistic to those who do, a place where monsters dwell, with obstacles and illusions to waylay adventurers, and whose very walls can be a force of corruption. It is a haunted place, ever at the edge of sanity.

THE MOLE TRAIN

Chapter One

I climb out of the subway in my rented tuxedo. Midnight, still raining. It's five blocks from Astor Place station to East Seventh Street and unless I can suspend the laws of time and space I'll be late for my midnight meeting. I hope my client is understanding. I need this gig. Otherwise, when Jennifer files for divorce, I'll end up driving a cab.

The crowds in the East Village are thick and noisy as usual, in spite of the weather. I'm the oldest guy on the street, pushing through the throng, getting dark looks. The only one not hunting a Thursday night party or looking to score drugs. My rented tux is getting wet.

I jog down Seventh Street toward Miss Lily's, not a restaurant I would have chosen. But my prospective client left a message this morning: 'Midnight meeting, urgent.' No word on how she found me. An odd message, the kind that, in happier times, I would have disregarded. These are not happier times.

I spent this Thursday evening trailing a suspected cheater to a gala at the Met, hence the tuxedo. The guy left early, a young fox not his wife hanging on his arm. I trailed them to a hotel five blocks away. A few iPhone shots of the couple entering a room on the eighth floor, an email to wifey, and I'm out of there, headed back to the East Village.

I hit Lily's front door at twelve-oh-seven. The clashing colors and jagged shapes on the cafe walls take me back a decade or so, to when I was a cop. The punk rock scene had swept the Lower East Side back then. We did our share of ridding the streets of scruffy, strung-out youths. I felt lucky I hadn't ended up that way myself.

The joint has calmed down a little since then, taken on a mellower Jamaican vibe. I spot a woman sitting by herself in a back booth. Pale green dress, nicely tailored, white scarf setting off the red hair. Laura Whitcomb, at least that's the name she gave me on the phone. Call me politically incorrect, but she is smokin' hot. Definitely uptown. She looks out of place amongst the diverse crowd of hipsters. And me, Vince Richards, large and white, wearing a tux, looking a little out of place myself.

My prospective client's expression is disconcertingly beatific. Maybe she's meditating. A medallion hangs around her neck on a leather thong. A pentacle. Shit. Prepare for a weirdo—a beautiful weirdo. Whatever she's doing, she looks good doing it. A few of the customers have noticed her as well and track me enviously as I approach her table.

She holds a Prada purse on her lap, all buckles and black leather. The scent of jasmine drifts around her. She smiles, holds out her hand. "Laura Whitcomb."

Her hand feels damp. A crack in her serene facade. I'll bet she doesn't have many. As our hands touch an odd sensation washes over me. I know this woman from somewhere. Maybe we were lovers in a past life, if there is such a thing.

"Vincent Richards. Call me Vince."

"Call me Laura." Five words and she's charmed me. The tone of her voice reminiscent of an old movie. I try to decipher the look in her eye. I hate all things woo-woo but there's kind of an aura about her. Her gaze is intense. I have to force myself to maintain eye contact. If I had hackles, they would be up. I remind myself she's a potential client.

I want to say, '*You called me,*' resist the urge, settle for, "Where did you get my name?"

Before she can answer, my phone chirps. My soon-to-be ex-wife has a gift for picking the worst goddamn time to call.

A frown creases Laura's lovely face."You have to get that? I'm in kind of a hurry."

I send the call to voicemail and slip the phone back in my pocket. "Why?"

"Someone is trying to kill me."

"I don't do bodyguard work."

"I don't need you for that. I have an ouanga bag for protection." She pulls a red brocaded pouch out of the Prada.

A magic bag—this one is checking off every box on the loony chart. I fight to keep a straight face. "How's that working out for you?"

"It's more complicated than that."

"So what *do* you want me to do?"

"I need you to find somebody."

"Who?"

Before she can answer, our waiter, skinny young guy in a white shirt and a black apron, bustles up, hands us menus. I know the jerked chicken is good, but I don't have much of an appetite. I hand the menu back.

He frowns, looks at Laura. "Ma'am?"

She shakes her head. "We won't be here that long."

"Just resting your feet?" he says with a New York sneer.

"Jerked chicken," I say. He walks off, mollified. "Is someone trying to kill you or not?"

"Destroy me. Destroy all of us."

The uh-oh beacon lights up my radar. "All of us, who?" I'm seeing a whole nest of crazies, now.

"Do you know anything about Wiccans?"

Yep, anything woo-woo in plural is bad. I sigh with resignation. "I don't do supernatural either."

"You're mocking me. They all are. It seems like something they feel compelled to do."

"Who's 'they'?"

"Evil forces."

"Like my first ex-wife?"

"You can't even imagine. Maybe I made a mistake coming here."

"I see your pentagram." I point at the medallion around her neck. "When you get hold of this guy you want me to find, what are you gonna do—"

She cuts me off. "Didn't say it was a guy."

"—cast a spell on him, her, it with your witch badge?"

Her eyes flash and I resist the urge to cringe. "The pentagram is a sacred symbol, whether you believe it or not."

Looks like she's revving up for a fight. I remind myself that I'm soon to be neck deep in financial alligators, raise my hands in a placating gesture. "Look, I don't know anything about you, except that you're afraid and that someone is threatening you. If you tell me what's going on, maybe I can help you." I clear my throat and do my best to sound convincing when I add, "I would really like to try."

The waiter shows up with my jerked chicken. "Everything all right here?"

"Fine," she says, meaning not fine.

My phone again. Jennifer. Tempted to ignore it, but I tap the button. "What?"

"Becky's acting out."

"What does that mean?" I ask.

"It's like she's in a trance, and there's this kind of moaning."

"Call nine-one-one."

"No, she's not sick, she's—"

Laura frowns, makes like she wants me to hand her my phone.

" I'll call you back." I drop the phone back in my pocket.

"That was about Becky, wasn't it?" she says.

The question hits me like a shot to the solar plexus. I force myself to take a deep breath. "How the hell could you know that?"

"Jennifer told me …"

"Jennifer? As in my wife, Jennifer?"

"She said—" Laura looks behind me. Her eyes widen. "It's too late. They've found us."

I turn around. A shape, indistinct in the shadows, slides toward me. I duck, but a dusting of powder hits me. My face is on fire, tears are streaming down my cheeks. I fall back in the booth, paw at my face, fight for breath. Everything goes black.

❧

A voice that sounds like the movie-trailer guy echoes in my head: "This is a time that is not a time. This is a place that is not a place." A train races past, light streaming from its windows. Dim images float in the darkness: A wagon creeping up a hill, a rope thrown over a branch. A human form swings in the evening shadows. A swirling montage of animal shapes: black dogs, red cats, yellow birds. Soft crying in the darkness.

❧

I open my eyes, take a shaky breath, still reeling from the vision of violent death. Laura Whitcomb is gone. My jerked chicken is cold. Our snotty waiter stands over me, hands me a check. "Nineteen dollars."

I give him a twenty and a five. My head aches, my face is still burning and I'm having trouble getting my breath. "How long was I out?"

"Maybe a couple of minutes."

"My chicken is stone cold. How did that happen?"

"You pass out and you're complaining about the temperature of your food?"

"And you just let me lie here?"

"I don't do domestic."

"Somebody hit me with some kind of knockout powder. You see that? This was not domestic."

The waiter looks around with a sigh, like he's reluctantly accessing memory banks. "There was a Spanish-looking guy in a hoodie when I was headed to the kitchen."

"Spanish-looking?"

"Yeah, I don't know. Skinny, pimples, loser, looking for a table. Gone when I came back. You were out, so maybe him. I thought you were drunk."

"Did I *look* drunk when I came in?"

Italian shrug.

I struggle out of the booth and stand on unsteady legs. "The red head, see where she went?"

He points over his shoulder towards the park across the street. "She left on the run. Kicked off her heels and booked it."

And none of this raised any alarms for you. I strive for calm. "The guy in the hoodie?"

Another shrug. "This is way farther into your business than I want to be. We'd appreciate you don't come back."

It's stopped raining. I dodge my way through traffic, cross the street into Tompkins Square Park, check my watch as I run: just after one a.m. Something is off. I met Laura at midnight. We talked for a couple of minutes, and the waiter said I was out only a couple of minutes. There's an hour unaccounted for or the waiter's full of shit.

Streetlights in the park cast shadows on the empty sidewalks under the famous Elm trees. Their branches glisten, liquescent from the rain. There seems no chance of finding Laura Whitcomb. She's had an hour to get ahead of me.

I call Jennifer, noting I've missed five calls from her. "What's going on with Becky?"

"She's been doing this kind of shaking—tremor thing. She's outside now, just staring down at the sidewalk. I'm scared, Vincent."

"Call an ambulance, for chrissake. I'll get there soon as I can."

"Try."

"I'll *try*." I walk into the park, holding the phone to my ear. "I have to ask you a question. Who's Laura Whitcomb?"

A pause. "Who?"

She's either forgotten or she's lying, but before I can call her on it, a guy in a long black coat, one of those waxed canvas numbers Australian cowboys wear, runs at me out of the darkness, knocking me off my feet. My phone goes flying. He's clutching a woman's purse. Prada. His eyes are wild. An odd little smile twists his face. His hair, matted with sweat, hangs over his forehead. All I get is a fleeting glance, but I'll recognize him if I see him again. He's missing his right ear.

My phone lies beside a puddle on the sidewalk. Miraculously, it still works. Jennifer's voice is a tinny squeak: "What happened? Where are you?"

I snatch it up. "Tompkins Square Park. I'll call you back."

"Wait. What the hell am I supposed to do?" I shut off the phone and walk farther into the park, something no one dared do a few years ago, not at one in the morning. The central plaza is deserted. In the leaf-dappled shade of an elm tree, Laura Whitcomb's body hangs from a branch by a rope.

Chapter Two

Her feet dangle just off the ground. I throw my arms around her legs, and lift her, trying to take the pressure off her neck. Her body is warm but I feel her dead weight. Her face is pale in the unforgiving streetlight. Her eyes, devoid of the life they had in the café, stare straight down at me. I'm too late.

Her pentagram rests against her coat. Her woo-woo did not protect her.

I want to drop her and run but I hang on, keeping slack in the rope, knowing it won't help her. Something crinkles in her coat pocket. I reach in, pull out a crumpled note, stuff it in my pocket. I study the noose. Thirteen coils, knot tight behind her right ear. Her hangman knew his work.

A voice behind me. "Show me your hands."

I consider ignoring him, but I know how this must look to a cop. I raise my hands.

"Turn around."

Two undercovers, hard eyes, scruffy street clothes. One approaches, stocking cap pulled low on his forehead.

He holds a badge in his left hand, gun in his right. Number two stands out of my line of sight, back in the shadows. They've done this before.

"Lay your gun on the ground."

"It's licensed."

"Sure it is. On the ground."

I lift my Beretta out of its holster with thumb and forefinger and lay it on the cobbles.

"Hands behind your head." His gun steady on my center mass.

"I didn't kill her."

"Shut up."

I manufacture a smile. "You guys from the Ninth?"

"You trying to tell me you're on the job? He puts away his badge, holds out his hand. "Show me some I.D."

"License in my wallet. I'm a private investigator."

"Oh, goodie." His partner picks up my gun. Stocking cap studies my credentials. Over his shoulder, he says, "Vincent Richards."

His partner pulls out a cell phone.

"Call Georgia Flores," I say.

"Who's that?"

"She's one of your lieutenants."

"You mean 'George.'" The partner fights back a smirk as he talks into his phone. Asshole. Siren coming down Seventh.

Stocking cap steps up, checks Laura's pulse. "She's dead."

No shit.

His partner says, "Why'd you kill her?"

"Christ, can't you get her down off of there?"

A cruiser pulls up. Two uniforms, a male and a female, climb out, walk up to the undercover guys, ignoring me. The female officer says, "Lieutenant Flores wants to talk to your suspect. She says keep him on ice."

"Get the woman down," I say.

Lady uniform clicks handcuffs on me, shoves me into the cruiser's back seat.

I keep hollering at them but I'm talking to myself behind the locked door. A guy with a camera bag over his shoulders rides up on a bicycle, starts taking pictures. Funny he's all by himself. Maybe he got a tip. The cops make a grab for him, but he pedals away into the darkness, carrying tomorrow's probable front page on his sim card. Wonderful.

An ambulance arrives, lights and siren, drives over the curb and paramedics pile out, burly guys in dark blue coveralls. A brief consultation with the cops, then they're on a ladder cutting the rope. They lift Laura Whitcomb's mortal remains down and strap it on a gurney. Ambulance leaves sans siren. No hurry now.

Crime scene van pulls up. White coverall guys set up lights, open their kits. Stuff the noose in a clear plastic evidence bag. Time passes like a snail on a razor blade. Yellow tape stretches around this corner of the park. A crowd gathers.

An unmarked Crown Vic slides in next to the cruiser. My old partner has arrived.

Georgia Flores climbs out of the unmarked and slips into the cruiser's back seat beside me. It's almost two in the morning, but her makeup is fresh and every hair is in place. White blouse, black blazer. She's a good-looking woman, a trait she is not above exploiting with the men of the Ninth precinct. She glances at my tux. "A well-dressed killer." Then she's all business. "What happened here, Vincent?"

"Nice to see you, too, George." In the seven years I've know her, I've never heard anyone but me call her 'Georgia,' and I only did it once.

"I'm guessing you didn't string that woman up."

For some reason this hits me wrong. Some of our old friction points are still raw. "Nobody 'strung her up.' This is not Dodge fuckin' City. She was hanged, and no, I didn't do it. Thanks for the benefit of the doubt. I guess seven years counts for *something*." We're right back on the verge of arguing over nothing, like an old married couple.

She takes out a notebook, flips open the cover and pulls out a fountain pen. Montblanc, gold-plated tip. I gave it to her for Christmas one year when I had money. "Let's have it."

I start with the meeting at Lily's, tell her about the powder, the guy in the hoodie the waiter told me about, my trip to the park and the guy in the trench coat who knocked me over.

"You saw a suspect fleeing the scene and you're just telling us now?"

"Your undercover pals were not interested."

She shoots me a look, punches numbers on her phone. The trench coat guy's description will be out on the street in minutes but it's probably too late. "Your client give you a name?" she asks.

I tell my first lie. "She never got around to it."

She looks at me, writes something in her notebook. "You tamper with my crime scene?"

I think of the crumpled-up paper in my pocket and tell lie number two. "No."

Another stare, an expression I've seen on Flores' face a hundred times, I always called it her 'felony dead eye.' It's usually directed at a dirt bag suspect, said dirt bag tonight being me.

She slides out of the car, leaving me to mull things over. Her perfume lingers, but I'm not feeling romantic. However, when I see her talking on the phone, fine-tuned frame outlined in the crime scene lights, I feel a tingle. The park is crawling with cops, the crowd of watchers has grown, crowding in to get a look at the perp in the back seat of the cop car.

Why am I withholding information? Which is a felony by the way. I have to admit—I want this case for myself. My face still burns from the knockout powder hoodie-boy threw in my face. I will have a heart-to-heart with that alleged dirt bag.

Laura Whitcomb didn't deserve to die like that. Nobody does. My wife knows something, but I'd rather ask her myself than send cops after her. Jennifer has enough trouble with our daughter at the moment. Child rearing isn't a strong suit for either of us. I wonder what the hell the moaning is about. Is Becky going crazy? I can't think about it. It's like a cop convention outside. Domestic will have to wait. Like I told the waiter, this isn't domestic.

The cops, when they find out about Laura's witch connection, are likely to write this off as a kook killing, of which there are plenty in Manhattan. Flores is proud of her closure rate. Blowing this won't be an option.

Media vans are pulling up now, cops holding them back, which only makes them more persistent. Thompson's Square Park is lit up like a carnival. Flores pushes her way through the mob and ducks back into the car. "Makings of a first-rate bear-fuck," she says. Ms. Obvious, one thing that always irritated me.

"When can I get out of here?"

"Captain likes you for this."

"What did you tell him?"

Flores says, "We have a victim with no I.D, we have two mysterious men in black that only you have seen. You had your arms around the body when the undercovers got here." She holds up her hand, putting off my objection. "I know, you were holding her up, trying to save her. But you can see how that looks. Plus, I've known you long enough to know there's stuff you're not telling me. And it's pissing me off."

"I told you what happened. And when you hang somebody you don't stand there holding them up, wearing a fucking tuxedo."

"Nothing to add? You've had some time to think it over."

"You have it all." I did forget to mention overcoat guy was carrying Laura's purse, and probably her identification. If Witches carry I.D.

She shrugs. "Fine, we'll play it your way." She steps out of the cruiser and motions to the uniforms. Nobody says a word all the way to the station.

❧

The 9th precinct headquarters on the Lower East side is immediately recognizable to old-time TV watchers. It served as a background shot for the TV series, "Hill Street Blues." I walked through that front door a thousand times during the seven years I worked there. Never did see Sipowitz. This morning, just after three-thirty, I was escorted, for the first time, through a steel door around the side, in handcuffs.

My first time in a cell in this jail, my second time in jail. The first time I was a surf bum in Santa Monica. That night, well into my second six-pack, racing my beat-to-shit old Mustang up the Coast Highway, speed augmented by my then-favorite controlled substance. They clocked me at a hundred. Those were the days, my friend.

I share the holding pen with half a dozen other guys. A dusty light bulb in a steel mesh cage overhead paints all of us in a dirty yellow glow. Several of my cellmates are passed out, two are crying and the rest stare at me with cold jail-house malice. I stare back until most look away. All but a skinny dude with a shaved head and a neat little moustache who keeps eyeing me. He sits hugging his knees, a faint smile on his face. I ignore him. His eyes stay locked on me in a wide-eyed stare. I glance back at him. He nods. I scowl. Not tonight, punk.

He scratches his head, goes back to hugging his knees, still staring. The usual clangings and bangings echo around me. Sleep is out of the question, so I sit myself in a corner away from the bald guy and try to think.

I promised to call Jennifer back, but they took my cell before I got the chance. Nobody answered when I called from the payphone downstairs. Maybe she's taken Becky to the hospital. I'll try again in the morning. This will be a long night for her.

I play the evening over in my mind. Problem one is the witch thing. I know nothing about people like that; I've always thought of them as harmless kooks. It's hard to imagine enemies who blow nerve agents in people's faces and hang them expertly in a public park in the middle of the night. Obviously they followed Laura to our meeting and were prepped for the hanging. Whoever planned that had a real serious mad on. What could someone like Laura Whitcomb have possibly done to piss somebody off that bad?

I think about the weird fever dream I had when I was out. I'm not a believer in any kind of supernatural beings, but that was a damn strange montage, which I can't ignore, included some kind of lynching *before* I found Laura hanged. And somehow, I'd lost an hour. The waiter's "few minutes" made less and less sense. All that time, my daughter was having some kind of fit. Quite a string of coincidences, but what else could they be?

As the night drags on and sleep eludes me, sitting there in the dirty yellow light, I rehash the hanging. Nobody could have put that together on the spur of the moment. If the bad guys had just wanted to kill her, there were a hell of a lot easier ways. They crafted a professional noose, threw it over a tree in a public park. I remember the photographer just happening along. Maybe Laura's hanging was supposed to set some kind of example, send some kind of message. But for who?

I can't help wondering about my impulse to lie to George. Commit a felony, contaminate a crime scene, cover up the identity of the victim—that would surely impede the investigation. I'd known Laura Whitcomb less than twenty minutes but I felt a bond with her I couldn't explain to myself. Seeing her dead in the park had knocked me off my game, sent me hard down a path for revenge. Not like me to get emotionally involved. How had that happened?

You hear about people looking into your soul—that was Laura. I remember the intensity in her green eyes. She would have made a hell of an interrogator, at least as good as George, who had figured out in thirty seconds I was fudging my story. I knew she'd come back at me in the morning.

Whatever was going on I had to keep Jennifer out of it. My wife had known Laura, and Laura had known about Becky. I need to find out about that. I'd had little contact since Jennifer and I separated. She lived down on the Lower East Side, had a new job, a store clerk of some kind. Her income cut down my support payments a little.

Those quiet hours just before dawn are when most people commit suicide. All the demons in your life c ollect around you in the darkness. I wasn't at that point yet, but I sit on the concrete floor, my eyes closed, feeling a nameless fear grow in me. It seems like hours, but it was probably only a few minutes. Don't know if I slept or not.

Foremost on my mind is Becky. Did she have a seizure, some kind of stroke? Do kids have strokes? I should have read the child-raising books we bought. If I were a praying kind of guy, this would be a good time.

Terrible scenarios play out in my head, driven by a nightmarish sound track of screams and shouts and banging cell doors. Some guy down the corridor is kicking his cell door over and over. I feel his frustration and rage. I picture my daughter strapped down in some kind of white room, mind destroyed, staring at the ceiling, seeing monsters in her head. I force the images out of my mind. The door-kicking guy doubles his efforts.

Jennifer and I had our share of scream-fests and broken crockery. Our daughter, Becky, in spite of all our reassurances, thought it was all her fault, as kids do. All we could think of was to separate. Probably for the best—for Becky's sake. What business do I have being a dad? Or a husband, for that matter. My eyes pop open. The bald guy stares at me, runs a finger over his lip, smoothing down his mustache. I want to smash his face but I turn away. Force myself to focus on the problem at hand. Whoever killed Laura Whitcomb can probably connect her to Jennifer. That puts my wife and daughter in danger. It's up to me to protect them, find whoever killed Laura Whitcomb.

The holding pen door slams open. "Richards, Vincent Richards."

Chapter Three

George says, "Sit down, Vince."

I follow her orders.

She turns on her digital recorder. Her mood is foul this morning. She's put together like she's going somewhere important. I'd think she climbed out of bed with her hair and make-up perfect, if I didn't know better.

It's seven in the morning and I'm barely awake, having spent a mostly sleepless night in the noise factory that is the ninth precinct jail, and stumbling down the long, dark road of self-examination. She recites our names and the date for the recorder, standard procedure. Feels a lot different on the other side of the table.

I try not to look surprised when she plops a black Prada handbag on the interrogation room table. She studies me, waiting for a reaction. She's good at that. I wipe all the expression off my face. I like to think I'm good at that. When she gets no reaction, she says, "Mr. Richards, who is Valerie Park?"

The question surprises me, but this time I don't have to lie. "I have no idea."

"You ever see this purse before?"

I shrug. "Lot of Prada out there."

She switches off the recorder. "You have to help me out here, Vincent. We found this bag a block from the crime scene, stuffed in a dumpster. A wallet in it. Driver's license had the deceased's picture on it, identifying her as Valerie Park. Thing is, there is no Valerie Park in the state of New York or any other state in the country that comes close to matching our victim. She looked like an affluent person, not some street bum, but, unless she's been living in a cave somewhere off the grid, the license is fake. The address is a vacant lot in Brooklyn. So we have a Jane Doe here."

Or we have Laura Whitcomb. First rule of lying, tell as much of the truth as possible. "The woman you found in the park was carrying that purse when we met in the café."

"And she didn't identify herself?"

"Never heard her say, 'Valerie Park.'"

"That's a non-answer. I can arrest you if you're withholding evidence."

After a brief staring contest, she turns the recorder back on. I repeat the story about seeing the purse. I leave out the part about trench coat guy carrying it out of the park, repeat the lie about not hearing her identify herself. I'm nailed on the record now.

She says, "I'm not going to arrest you. We checked out your story at the café. No way you could have run across the street and tied a rope around her neck and did an expert hanging job on our Jane Doe. You were a pretty good cop. I don't see you doing that. But this is not over."

"So don't leave town?"

"Don't be a smart ass. We'll know more tomorrow."

"You'll let me know?"

A sigh. She shuts off the recorder. "Know that I think? I think you know more than you're telling. I think you want this yourself. Maybe somebody set you up, maybe you're pissed about whatever the powder was they threw in your face. We'll have the tox screen back later. Something exotic, they said in the lab, but they'll figure it out. Let us handle this."

I push my chair back. "You had me at, 'I'm not going to arrest you.'"

She pulls a medallion out of a manila envelope on the table, the pentagram I saw around Laura Whitcomb's neck. "What do you make of this?"

"You're channeling Colombo: 'Just one more thing.'"

"This, and the powder thing make me wonder if you're getting into a little black magic."

"Truth is I have no idea what I'm getting into. And there is no such thing as magic."

"You really believe that?"

"You don't?"

"Just don't get in my way. I want to close this case—I need to close this case."

That admission had to be hard for her. I know how hard she's had to struggle in the macho world of cops. Everyone is rooting for her to fuck up. I feel sorry for her. She's been fighting that battle for ten years.

"The media are getting loud," she says. "There's a picture of our Jane Doe on the front page of the *Times* this morning. Caption is, 'Mystery Woman Hanged in Park.' Picture went viral. The captain is not happy."

"At least they didn't say, 'witch hanged.'"

"You gotta help me out, Vincent, for old time's sake."

"We had some times, didn't we?" She looks up from her yellow pad, but doesn't comment.

We finally come to a resolution of sorts. We'll keep each other informed. I promise not to get in the way of her investigation. We will keep our communication under the radar. I mess up, and I'm still good for obstruction of justice. She walks out of the interrogation room with just a quick glance over her shoulder. A damn attractive woman. I wonder if she, like me, ever thinks about what might have been.

❧

First light in Flatbush.

The Haitian Voodoo priestess, Augusta Louventure, who has taken to calling herself Madam Augusta, flexes her hands, watches the sinews wind and twist under the skin. She makes a fist, smiles as her fingers dig into her palms, welcoming the pain. Still strong, still power there. No one will take that from her, not the cartels, not the weird little fairies who flit around waving their burning bundles of sage. She drops down onto the carpet, knocks off fifty pushups. Madam Augusta still has it.

But she has far more power than that residing in her body. She has the power of the ancient ones—the Spirits that surround her everywhere—a power that reaches through space to reward or punish. The mysterious force called voodoo. Symbols of that power are everywhere in this wide-open living room she calls her office. Pictures cover every wall: her children, movie stars and Catholic saints. The mantle of a long-defunct fireplace is cluttered with dolls, feather flowers, miniature dishes.

Over the door hangs a voodoo charm to protect the family. Next to it hangs a horseshoe entwined with a Palm Sunday cross. Incense smolders in a brass bowl beside her chair. A red and blue scarf hanging over the window tempers the morning light, giving the room a murky, mysterious air. Just as Madam Augusta prefers. Just as the Spirits prefer.

As a child back in Haiti, Augusta Louventure had dreams of riding a mighty train. Harnessing a magical dark force. The vision came back to her from time to time over the years when the Spirits inhabited her body. Words flashed before her eyes in the darkness, naming that dark force: "Labirent tren." She could not be sure of the meaning of these words in the Creole dialect, only that they were the key to unleashing the power that would make her dreams come true. She had had the words tattooed on her shoulder. She lays her fingers on the tattoo now and gives herself over to the power of the spirits.

She smiles at the pleasure it brings her as the vision appears again: steel wheels rumbling along the track, smokestack throwing clouds into the sky. From her window seat she watches the world flash by. Far away, past the slums of Port Au Prince, into kingdoms of stellar light. And now, her dream is about to come true, bringing wealth, respect from a cold, unforgiving world. Evening the score. She feels herself transported to a higher plane.

This dream stayed with her to the United States, but father and husband ran things, paid little attention to her, intent only on their drug enterprises. When they were murdered, she became the leader and could begin to follow her mystical dream. She heard rumors of a magical train running under the streets of Manhattan. They called it an urban legend. But Madam Augusta knew it was true. She rode it.

The Spirits visited her some months before while she was in a trance seeking guidance for her bold new venture. She was transported to another place and time, a dark, evil place where people lost their minds and women were hanged for their sins. No one understood what was happening, the seeds of their madness were buried deep under the earth—deep in their human spirits. And in this dark space, a great secret—and a great power—lay.

Madam Augusta, floating that night in a semi-conscious state, implored the Spirits. "Show me." She found herself facing a blinding light. A deep-throated roar overwhelmed her. A hot wind rushed over her and she fell onto her back as a powerful *something* rushed over her. Do not be afraid, the Spirits told her.

A symbol floated in front of her eyes: A pentagram. The five points of the star glowed with pale fire. To Wiccans, the star symbolized the four elements of air, water, earth and fire, perfectly balanced to create the fifth element of spirit. The message was clear: These people held the key to the power. The key to the *labirent tren.*

When she awakened from the trance, Madam Augusta swore to herself, and to her Spirits, that the Wiccans would relinquish that power to her—or she would tear it from them. But it was not clear how she might harness it to promote her drug empire. Again, she approached the Spirits, and the next night, she got the answer: In this vision she is onboard the mysterious train, sitting beside a woman in a long white dress. She realizes the woman is dead. Images flash by the windows in blinding progression: Sky scrapers set against the craggy peaks of the Andes. The skyline of Bogota, Columbia. A rust-red archway towering above a garbage-littered street. The Iron

Market in Port Au Prince. The bulbous turrets of Red Square, the Empire State Building. She realizes, insane as it seems, she's being transported around the world in an instant. It's the perfect delivery system.

She doesn't tell her sons. They would laugh at her behind her back; she knows they do, but she pays them no attention. They call her crazy, with all her spells and incantations, but this morning, when her children come back, she will show them—with her power—the price of disobedience. With the power of the Spirits behind her, she will soon control this whole sinful New York town. Then no man will ever laugh behind her back again. Maybe then she can reveal to these doubters her perfect delivery system.

Her youngest son, Wilky, is the first up the stairs, strutting with the bravado that comes only from youth. "We've done it," Wilky Mouton says. "She's dead." How proud is his carriage, how proudly he bears his father's name.

"I know. You told me," Madam Augusta says. "Now tell me what happened after that."

Wilky's brother, the tall young Haitian named Little Jay, comes up behind him and takes off his hoody. "I explain. A cop came into the park. I almost ran over him but he fell down and I got away."

"But you didn't get her purse?"

"There was a problem. Some guys jumped me as I get on my bike. They take it away."

Madam Augusta rises from the brocade chair that serves as her throne, paces slowly toward Little Jay. "And you have nothing that was hers, nothing that will give me the power over her? You think a rope can kill this kind of woman? I need something of hers, I must control her soul!"

Little Jay shrugs. Madam Augusta shakes her head. "You fool." She grabs his shoulders. He stands paralyzed, too frightened to flee. Her fingers dig into his flesh. She squeezes harder. His eyes widen. He convulses and collapses on the rug.

Wilky steps forward trembling. "There's one thing. The cop Little Jay ran into? He was not a cop, he was the man the Priestess met in Miss Lily's." He screws his face into a smile. "Some of my powder must have missed him." He holds up his hand. "Don't hurt me."

Madam Augusta sits back in her chair, closes her eyes. "He is alive?"

A faint squeak that might have been a 'yes.'

"You will find him and make it right. Or, son or no son, you will join this one." She pokes Little Jay's trembling form with the toe of her sandal. His incompetence may be a sign that her spirit power is weakening. It's time to renew their energy. Time to visit the Greenwood Cemetery. To offer a living sacrifice.

Chapter Four

Outside the 9th Precinct I pull out my cell phone. Ten-percent left. I call Jennifer. No answer. At the beep, I say, "It's Vincent, pick up if you're there. Is Becky all right?" I start up First Avenue toward my apartment, a sense of dread building in my head, reimagining the scenarios that kept me up all night.

I am so distracted by my thoughts it takes me three blocks to realize I'm being followed. By somebody who isn't very good at it. I wait at a light on Eighth Street and, out of long habit, make a quick look back, making like I've forgotten something. My tail, a young Hispanic guy in a flowered shirt, stops short and bends to tie his shoe. Only his sandals have no laces. Where do they get these guys?

He has to be connected to Laura Whitcomb's murder. Maybe even the one who threw the powder at me. An old saying comes to mind, "They have me surrounded, the poor bastards." I continue my stroll up First Avenue, giving no sign that I've spotted him. My apartment is on Twelfth Street, a couple of blocks ahead. I have an advantage here. I grew up in this neighborhood, still live in the apartment my mother left me when she died two years ago.

Up the street is a tennis court behind an iron fence. The gate is unlocked, as it always has been. I turn in, walk across the court into an alley, one of my favorite childhood hideouts. There's a recessed doorway about half-way down. I slip inside and wait, back pressed against the bricks. Flower shirt peeks in the alley, pulls a knife out of his pocket and takes a cautious step inside. He slips past my doorway, sees me a second too late. I twist the knife out of his hand, spin him toward me and slam my heel down on his instep. Bones grind together. He cries out, slumps in my arms.

"You a dead man." Trying to sound like Mister Tough Guy.

I swat him in the head. Tough Guy curls himself into a ball and lies there whimpering. I call George. Up to her now. I can't detain and interrogate civilians, as much fun as that might be. She picks up on the first ring. "Flores."

"I have a suspect for you," I tell her. "It might be our powder-thrower."

"Don't hurt him."

"He fell down and hurt himself." I explain that he followed me from the station, give her our location. "Come and get him. I don't think he's going anywhere."

"You willing to press charges?"

"My phone is dying. I'll talk to you later."

"Vincent, goddamnit."

The walk back to my apartment makes me feel like I'm walking point somewhere on a dirt road outside Kabul. Everybody looks suspicious. My adrenaline is boiling, the way a man coming at you with a knife makes it do. I'll be readier next time. I keep an eye on my back trail, scenting the wind. At least I didn't lead the scumbag to my apartment. My place on East Twelfth is not fancy. A third-floor walkup. Two bedrooms. I'd shared the place with my mom for most of the time I was in New York. She willed it to me. Otherwise I could never have afforded it.

I walk past the door, cross the street and watch for a while. Nobody shows any interest. I cross back and climb the stairs. My so-called bachelor pad is over-decorated with my Mom's wild-ass modernistic paintings. Done during the hectic punk-rock days when her fame was at its height. Back when I was married and living in L.A. with Jennifer.

Later, after Mom died, Jennifer and I moved to New York and lived here for two years until she took Becky and moved out. Didn't bother to tell me where she was going. I converted the apartment to a bachelor pad, earth tones and leather furniture. I kept the long glass table my Mom loved so much. I remember how she entertained all her artist friends around it, drinking tequila and eating her famous Mexican casserole. Jennifer and I shared many a Thai take-out there.

That thought prompts me to call my ex. No answer. I tell myself it's not really my problem but the bullshit monitor chirps in my head. Becky is *our* daughter. That's something that will never change. She's thirteen, going on twenty-five. She's put away her school science projects, her dreams of being a cop, following in dad's footsteps, and morphed into an angry, acting-out teen.

My phone beeps a final warning and flat-lines, out of power. I give up, put it on the charger, lie down on the bed and try to recover from my jail-house all-nighter. Three hours later, I'm out of the shower and putting on coffee when my rejuvenated phone rings.

George believes preambles waste her time. "Your knife guy is Wilky Mouton, Haitian national. Low level drug dealer. In the hospital getting his foot put in a cast."

"Tell you anything?"

"Tough punk. Told us nothing. Threatens to sue."

"After coming after me with a knife?" Water is boiling. I pour it into the French Press, let it steep.

"You're making coffee, aren't you?"

She knows me too well.

"Narcotics knows about Mr. Mouton," she says. "And the news isn't good. They think he's connected to The Baka."

The name triggers an unpleasant memory. The people that killed my partner back in my patrol days. "Miami street gang. Nasty bunch."

"Apparently, they're back, trying to make some inroads into selling in New York."

"Just what we need."

I hear a rustling noise on the phone. Phone tucked into her shoulder, George is drawing her hair back into a bun so it doesn't get grabbed by a dirt bag. Doing her 'getting ready for the street' ritual. I've seen her do it a hundred times. Looks kind of sexy. Next she'll pull out her Glock and check it. I hear the clicks. She says, "Leader is rumored to be a woman. Some kind of Haitian voodoo princess calling herself 'Madam Augusta.'"

"So, what's the bottom line? Do we know Wilky is connected to the Haitian guys?"

"Not yet, but that's the way to bet. Here's another bit of news. Your Jane Doe didn't die from being hanged. She was dead when they strung her up."

"Why hang a dead woman?"

"The point of hanging her in such a prominent place, and tipping off a photographer, is to send a message."

"To who? Our Jane Doe doesn't strike me as a gang leader."

"No. If her little pendant is any indication, she's a witch." She chuckled.

"Wearing a pentagram doesn't make you a witch. And as for a Haitian gang declaring war on witches, even you must recognize that this is crazy shit."

"Here's where the gang connection comes in," she says. "M.E. says her bloodstream was loaded with something called *coupe poudre*. The chemical name is 'tetrodotoxin.' Zombie powder."

"Zombies. Jesus. Listen, I gotta go. My ex called me last night to tell me my daughter was having some kind of mental problems."

George is not interested in my domestic situation. I don't think she ever liked Jennifer. Never knew why. "Take care of your business, Vincent. Leave the Haitians to us. These gang guys are serious crazies."

"Why are they following me, trying to knife me in the street?"

"No idea. Maybe it's your attitude."

"You know I can't let this go?" I say.

"I do, unfortunately." She hangs up.

I make myself some lunch, pancakes and eggs. For some reason, I'm putting off another call to Jennifer. Maybe avoiding my responsibilities. Maybe just hoping she had already taken care of Becky's problem. Surely if anything horrible had happened, she would have called me, wouldn't she?

A lot had happened since Jennifer and I separated a year ago. I hung out my PI shingle and she went back into the work force, got a job but didn't tell me what or where. We hadn't seen each other much since. She thought my job was a bad influence on Becky, glorifying violence and all that stuff. I disagreed but there was no point in arguing. Our breakup was about more than that. Different dreams, you could say. I put all that out of my mind for the moment, focus on the business at hand. Somebody wants me dead, someone who probably knows I met Laura Whitcomb.

I wash my dishes, put them on the rack to dry. Wipe down my glass table. Stare out the window. Nobody down on the street shows any particular interest in my apartment. Finally, my worry gets the better of me and I pick up the phone, call Jennifer to find out what's happening with Becky. And there's another question I'm dying to ask. Why did she deny knowing Laura Whitcomb?

Chapter Five

Since our separation a year ago, Jennifer and I have mostly communicated by phone. Not comfortable being in each other's presence. Jennifer picks up after half-a-dozen rings. Lot of noise in the background, people talking, thumping around like someone moving boxes.

"Been trying to reach you," I say.

"Becky is okay, thank you for asking." Pissy right out of the gate.

"Check your messages once in a while." Pissy right back. The old tapes play on.

"I've been swamped here all morning." Her acidic tone tells me all I need to know about her mood.

"What happened?" I ask.

"She finally quieted down, put on her headphones and disappeared back into her music. Like nothing happened. She wouldn't talk to me, but that's nothing new. I don't know if she's into drugs or … I can't talk about this now. I'm not supposed to take personal calls at work."

I hear the strain in her voice and it triggers a guilt reflex in me. I resolve to help her with Becky, whatever that means. She's right, this isn't the time for an in-depth family discussion. But I have to be realistic. Becky's back to normal for the moment, but there are other threats to her and Jennifer on the horizon. Things I *can* do something about.

"I understand how you feel, Jennifer."

"I doubt that, but we're going to have to work this out somehow."

"I need to see you. Can we meet?"

"Why?"

"A couple of things to clear up. Starting with, where are you?"

We wrangle back and forth for a few minutes until she finally agrees to meet me, though I can tell she really doesn't want to. She tells me she has taken a job at an occult supply shop called The Enchantress as some kind of stock girl—stock person—on East 9th street. This occult bit sends a chill through me. The unexplainables are piling up. Starting to get creepy. How many witches are hanging around this case?

I hang up and call a ride share. The car, a black, late-model Audi, pulls up in front of my apartment building. The driver turns his head away, checking his mirror as I climb in the back. He looks familiar, but there are a lot of Uber drivers in the city. Not all of them shave their heads, however.

"You got here in a hurry," I say.

"We're burning daylight." His voice is low, muffled. It's a movie directors' line. Not particularly appropriate for the moment, but I don't want to exchange idle banter with some hired driver. I ignore him.

He has Jennifer's work address in his computer so there's no need for further communication. He cuts into traffic and heads down 12th street without another word.

He double-parks in front of The Enchantress. I hop out and hand him a couple of bills. He doesn't look at me, but I catch sight of his face in his rear-view mirror. He looks a little like the bald guy in my cell the night before, mustache and all. He smoothes it with his finger. Before I can get a closer look the car slides away down the street. Its waxed, black fenders glow in the afternoon light.

I put the driver out of my mind and peer in The Enchantress's front window, check out the displays of tarot cards, talismans, oils, incense, and herbs and resins. Several women customers stare at me.

Jennifer walks out of the back room carrying boxes. Her hair-do fits right in. Pale pink, half her head shaved, the other half an irregular clump of frizz. Bit of a change from the So-Cal surfer honey I fell in love with, followed blindly across the country ten years ago. My golden girl has gone to the other side, the dark side maybe.

She notices me, not looking happy. I smile and wave. She says something to the women customers. They nod in agreement, turn their frowns on me. I imagine their conversation: Men are scum. She shakes her head and points down the street, meaning meet me there.

I wait for her in a recessed doorway. Finally she walks toward me. A lot of my old feelings come back, but her old free-swinging stride is gone, her steps are tight, cramped. She's wearing a long white skirt and a blue peasant blouse embroidered with flowers and twining vines. It clashes with her pink hair, but what do I know? She's still a fine-looking woman, but I know enough not to let her physical appearance cloud my vision. I've seen too much of the other side of her. We can never get back on the same page, if we ever were on the same page. She's best viewed at a distance.

But seeing her again makes me think of Becky. Jennifer, even in her post-modern pre-punk hairdo, is the adult image of our daughter. I remember taking the kid to the beach and to the park, and reading her stories to put her to sleep. She gave me that little smile and patted me on the nose like I was her puppy, I just fell apart. First time she did it, I cried. She asked, "Did I hurt you, Daddy?"

"Daddy," she said in that cute, little kid voice. I fight tears now as her mother walks toward me. Don't get me wrong, Jennifer is a good person, vibrant, outgoing, in love with the world. She's just not in love with me.

I haven't seen her in almost a year. She looks over her shoulder now, worried expression on her face. Her eyes are red. With her honey-blonde ponytail replaced by pink fuzz, she looks undone. No wonder, worrying about a sick kid all night.

"You get any sleep last night?" I ask.

"Thanks, you look like hell yourself. Got a neurologist appointment for Becky. Ten o'clock tomorrow if you can make it." I copy the address into my phone. We step back into a doorway like characters in a bad spy book.

"How do you know Laura Whitcomb?" I ask.

"Who says I do?"

"She does … she did. She's dead."

Jennifer's hand flies to her mouth and her eyes tear up. "She can't be."

"I saw her body—unless there's something I don't know."

"There are a lot of things you don't know."

I tell her about meeting Laura at Miss Lily's. "She said you recommended her, mentioned you by name."

Jennifer says, "That was supposed to be a secret."

I run through the rest of the story, the toxic powder, the missing hour, and finally, finding Laura Whitcomb's body in the park.

Jennifer's eyes widen. Fresh tears. "They *hung* her?"

"Who is *they*?"

She crowds herself further back into the doorway, scans the street, looking for something. I glance over my shoulder. Three women waiting for the light, deep in conversation. A skateboarder. Some guy in a blue and white stocking cap unlocking his bike. Nothing out of the ordinary.

"Now we're all in danger," she says.

"Who's *we*?"

"I can't …" She leans in, lowers her voice. "The coven."

"Coven? What the hell are you into here?"

Instead of answering, she pulls out her phone, punches a number. "I need a car. Soon as you can." She tucks the phone away.

"Talk to me, dammit. Where are you going?"

"I'm leaving, and if you're smart you'll do the same thing."

A car pulls up to the curb. Jennifer jumps in the back seat. I run toward the car, but it slides away from the curb and merges with the 9th Street traffic. A shiny black Audi. But somehow, polished as it is, the license plate is daubed with mud, unreadable.

The car stops at a light at the end of the block. I sprint after it, pushing my way through the crowd. The light changes, the Audi turns right onto Avenue B. When I get to the intersection, there's no sign of it. Things are going south faster than I can handle. Too much of a coincidence, the same ride share car suddenly appears to pick up Jennifer, arriving thirty seconds after she calls. My rational mind tells me the bald driver can't be the guy who shared the holding cell last night, the same guy who picked me up half-an-hour ago at my apartment.

My rational mind is fighting the notion that I've poked some kind of occult hornet's nest. But I'm beginning to suspect my rational mind might be slipping away. The guy who followed me from the jail was real enough. The knife he tried to stick in me was real enough and he has a real-enough broken foot for his efforts. Time to get my head out of the fog and focus on the reality of the streets around me.

A train whistle cuts through the street noise, followed by clatter of wheels on steel rails. The sound approaches, races past me and fades away with a final blast of the whistle. Lonesome, like some old country song. No one around me seems to notice.

So much for the reality of the streets. People are talking, some guy carries an old boom box along, jiving to Jimi Hendrix. A delivery van races its engine, the driver taps his horn, a cabbie gives him the finger. Everybody normal—but me.

I start across the street, make like I've forgotten something, spin around and hop back onto the curb. My clever little counter-surveillance dance has revealed that someone is, in fact, following me. A Crown Vic with black sidewalls idles at the curb. George, from her vantage point in the driver's seat, crooks her finger at me.

I slide into the front seat. "Still partnering with Little Stevie?"

That rates me a silent scowl. 'Little Stevie' is a thistle she calls her 'service plant,' her not-so-subtle way of mocking the unwashed who carry Chihuahuas and rabbits onto airplanes. The plant rides in her unmarked, in a gimbaled pot glued to the dash. I learned long ago not to touch it.

George blips her siren, clearing a space in traffic, and soon we're rolling north along Avenue B, the direction the Audi was traveling when last seen.

I relay that information to George. Her answer isn't helpful: "What Audi?"

"Hit your flashers. They can't be very far ahead."

"Who can't, Bonnie and Clyde?"

I explain my meeting with Jennifer, her disappearance in the ride share. George steps on the gas, picks up her hand mike. "License?"

I shake my head. "Covered with mud, couldn't read it."

A grimace. She hangs the mike back on the dash. "Seems to be a lot of things that only you've seen lately."

This is probably not a good time to mention the phantom train. The potted thistle dangling on her dash catches my eye. "Your plant is staring at me"

"When's the last time you saw your wife?"

"About ten minutes ago."

She rolls her eyes. "Before that?"

"A year or so. How is it the NYPD happened to show up just now?"

"So all of a sudden, after a year, you decide to go to her place of work and talk to her out on the sidewalk. What's the sudden urgency?" George is used to being the one asking the questions.

I try again, anyway. "How long have you been following me?"

"Watching your apartment."

"So you saw the ride share car that picked me up?"

"Come to think of it, a black Audi."

"You get a license?" I ask.

"Not doing your detective work for you. I think maybe your detecting skills are getting a little rusty. You didn't see the guy in the overcoat?"

I glance over my shoulder. "What guy?"

"Back at the occult shop? Sitting on a bench, pretending to read a book?"

I was so wound up talking to Jennifer, I missed the guy. Don't want to look too stupid so I take a calculated guess: "Wearing one of those canvas coats Australian cowboys wear? Of course I saw him." I couldn't tell her where I'd seen him before. The one-eared guy in the park. Last time he had a Prada purse under his arm.

Apparently it's a good guess because she says, "Ever see him before?"

I shrug.

She lets it go. "I spent some time talking to Narcotics this morning. There's a drug war brewing. Our park hanging is the third one this month. It's some Voodoo thing. Show of force."

"Who are the victims?"

"We're working on it."

Clearly, it's bugging her now that one of the cases is hers. I say, "Why are you tailing me?"

"You never did tell me why you suddenly decided to visit your estranged wife."

For once, I have a partial truth to tell her. "My daughter, Becky, had some kind of seizure last night. Jennifer was frantic. I came over to console her."

"How's the kid?"

"She's okay today."

"Let's connect a few dots here, Vincent." We cruise up Avenue B, dodging in and out of traffic. A slow-moving truck ahead. She taps the siren, we slip around it, pick up speed. Still no Audi.

"Take for example," she says, "the fact that our vic was wearing a Wiccan symbol, and your wife just happens to work in an occult shop, and you just happen to pay her a visit the day after the hanging, in spite of not seeing her for the past year. And then she hops in a ride share and takes off without you, in the same kind of car that delivered you to her workplace in the first place. And you chase her down the street. If you were in my shoes, wouldn't you be getting a little suspicious? Why don't you just spit it out."

"I can see where—"

"Vincent…" She has her stern cop expression on now, which strikes fear into the hearts of a lot of bad guys. "I know you're a tough guy, but you're messing with people who kill people. If your wife is involved with these people …" She leaves the thought unspoken. Nothing I haven't been worrying about for the past twelve hours. She says, "Time to tell me what the hell is going on."

Though I'm loath to drop a dime on my soon-to-be ex, the first rule of lying is, tell as much of the truth as possible. "Our hanging victim—"

She cuts me off. "My hanging victim."

"—was a customer in my soon-to-be ex-wife's store. Said she needed a private investigator. Jennifer recommended me. That's all there was to it."

"Why did she run away after you talked to her?"

I shrug. "Panicked."

She pulls to the curb. "Here's what's gonna happen. I will find your wife and I will question her. And if I find out you're holding out on me, I will bust your ass for obstruction, *claro*?"

"I love it when you talk Spanish."

"*Marchar*."

Chapter Six

By the time I walk half-a-block, my flippant, flirty, bullshit attitude collapses and I sink into an existential funk. I recognize that attitude for what it is: a defense mechanism, protecting me against what? Myself, more than likely. I resolve to knock it off and act like an adult.

The adult, former cop part of me, searches every face on the street, checks window reflections for a tail. The guy in the Australian coat is not in sight, or else he's changed his clothes. I focus on the reality around me, all the cars, the people moving along the street. I dash across Avenue A against the light. Several people, veterans of the New York street culture, dash with me. All of us get a flurry of horns and a forest of extended fingers. All of us ignore them. I stop and look back across the street. Nobody looking this way. My fellow crossers have melted into the crowd, heading their busy New York way.

I stand there for a moment absorbing the ambiance. I'm more than familiar with this part of town. I'm six blocks away from my apartment. It's an old familiar reality. But now, for the first time, I am beginning to sense there is something else going on. Some other reality? Outside my comfort zone, a feeling brought home by the phantom train nobody else heard.

Add up the strangeness of the past few hours, starting with the strange dream—or vision—whatever it was—when the powder hit me. I can still hear that theatrical trailer voice: *"This is a time that is not a time. This is a place that is not a place."* My first thought was to ignore this kind of enigmatic Zen bullshit. Now there seems to be some kind of eerie tie-in with the present reality. Main tie-in being the image I saw of a rope being thrown over a tree branch. This was before I knew about Laura Whitcomb hanging in Tompkins Square Park. I'm at a loss to explain the train I saw in my dream, the train I *heard*, racing past me on 9th Street, the swirl of animal shapes, all the different colors in my dreams. Forces are flowing through the East Village, aimed at doing harm to me and my family.

Somebody picked up Jennifer, likely the same black Audi ride share that picked me up. The driver looked a hell of a lot like the bald guy who, I am certain, shared a cell with me the night before. Jennifer called him outside the occult store and he showed up in less than a minute. She got in willingly and was gone. I can think of no explanation for that.

Jennifer knew Laura Whitcomb. But their connection wasn't clear. Maybe even my daughter was in the mix somehow, a thought that scared the shit out of me. But all I could really do was follow the clues, like any other investigation. Keep things in the realm of reality.

I am lost in thought as I reach my apartment building. I wake up when a tall man in a tailored black suit and a fedora pushes away from the wall and approaches me, hands in his pockets. Meeting Johnnie Tomasso is never good news.

We stop a yard apart and stand facing each other like gunfighters. I take the lead: "Something on your mind, Tommy-boy?"

"Always the smart ass, Vinny-boy. Nicknames piss me off, not to mention denigrating my proud Italian heritage. But forget the tough-guy bullshit. I have a proposition for you."

"'Denigrating.' Pretty fancy word for a thug."

"More with the insults. Listen up, this could be to your advantage, Richards."

"This some kind of 'or else' deal, Johnnie?"

"I'll ignore your tone of voice for now. What do you know about Haitians working in the city?"

"Probably underpaid."

He shifts his feet, looking like he's ready to make a move. Tomasso is a hitter for the mob, but I heard he was moving up into management. Probably not smart to provoke him any more than necessary to feed my ego. He takes his hands out of his pockets and I tense, wondering if I can jump him before he gets his gun out. He holds his hands toward me, palms out. "Relax, Vincent. If I wanted your ass, you'd be dead by now."

"So, if you don't want my ass, what do you want?"

"Certain people are a little concerned that there might be a new player trying to cut in on us. That will not happen. I know you've had some kind of contact with these people. Word is you put one of their street punks on crutches. So it's just possible we might be on the same side. So what do you know about some Haitians pushing pharmaceuticals here in the East Village?"

I thought about that. The cops considered the Haitians dangerous crazies. One of their people, Wilky, George said, was upset enough to come after me with a knife. It's likely they were responsible for hanging three people just to send somebody a message. The outfit is headed by some kind of Voodoo priestess.

"Nothing," I say.

"Here's the deal. You find these guys, you tell me." He hands me a card: Empire Enterprises. Raised letters, gold crest, a phone number. "We'll be watching you."

I tucked the card in my pocket. "What's in it for me?"

"You get to enjoy another day in the beautiful East Village."

"I'll think about it," I say.

He gives me a semi-friendly punch on the shoulder that knocks me back a foot. "You do that, Vincentie." A pristine white Escalade with black windows slides up to the curb. They must have some kind of a signal. He steps in, rolls down his window and points a thumb-and-finger gun at me as the SUV drives away. Subtle.

My phone rings as I'm riding the elevator back up to my apartment. Jennifer says with no preamble, "Becky's in the hospital."

"What happened? Where is she? How is she doing?"

She interrupts my stream of questions: "They took her to …" I hear paper rustling, "… the psychiatric inpatient unit on First Avenue." She reads me the address as I unlock my front door. I write it down on a pad on the kitchen counter.

She explains that Becky had some kind of mental breakdown. "They're keeping her for a day or two for observation. Doesn't seem to be anything physical wrong with her."

"My daughter is in a psychiatric hospital?"

"I've told you all I know. You can visit her."

"Damn right I'll visit her. Where are you?"

"I can't say right now."

"Where did you go in that ride share?"

"Can't tell you that either. You'll just have to trust me."

"The cops are looking for you."

"You sicced the cops on me?"

"Something a little strange is going on. We could all be in danger so please keep your eyes open." I slip on my shoulder rig and slide in the Beretta. "I'm going to see her. Meet you there?"

"I can't go right now."

The elevator comes. I jump in. "Why? You can't go see your own daughter?"

"They're taking care of her. It's just—awkward right now."

"I'll call you." I hang up, not waiting for her reply.

I dash out on the street, hail a cab. No more Uber, thanks. The cabbie pulls out onto 12th Street, paying no attention to his mirror. A thump behind us. Some guy on a bicycle, wife-beater shirt, blue-and-white stocking cap, picks up his bent bicycle, flips us the bird.

I zoom in on the stocking cap. "Better go back, maybe he's hurt."

The driver glances in his mirror, unconcerned. "Hit my cab? Fuck him." He stomps on the gas.

Life in the East Village.

▪

The reception desk at the psychiatric inpatient unit is staffed by two big, very serious-looking men in purple scrubs sitting behind a Plexiglas partition, like cashiers at a gas station in Brooklyn.

"Identification." The bigger of the two holds out his hand.

I hand over my P.I. license. He studies it. "Are you carrying a gun?"

I pull it out of the holster and slide it through the slot in the Plexiglas. "I'm Becky Richard's dad. I need to see her."

Big guy's partner picks up a phone, mutters into it. After a moment, he says, "She's resting. They can give you a few minutes."

No use getting in his face. He has procedures. They walk me along a windowless corridor to a nurse's station. Institutional gray linoleum, white walls, fluorescent-lit. Just beyond is a locked door with a chicken-wire glass window. I'm getting tense. My daughter is locked up in a mental hospital. There's a smell in the air, a contagious madness. If you aren't psychotic when you arrive you will be in an hour. How does the staff stand it?

A nurse in blue scrubs steps out from behind her desk. Big guys step back, flanking me. The nurse says, "A couple of things before I let you in. We've given her a sedative. They couldn't find anything physically wrong, but something frightened the hell out of her. You wouldn't know anything about, that would you?"

I should be pissed, but I can't blame her. I've seen enough abusive fathers in my cop days, hauled a few down their front steps kicking and screaming. Maybe I'm not guilty of anything, but, in this nurse's view, that's the way to bet.

"I love my daughter and I've never done anything to harm her. Her mother hasn't either."

"Where is the mother?"

"She'll be here in a little while." I shrug. "Traffic."

She gives a bullshit-detected look. "We'll see how it goes. Your daughter's in Room Fifteen."

The nurse punches some numbers in a pad on the door, opens it and leads the way, big guys close behind. The lighting beyond the door is low-key, fixtures recessed in the walls. The hall is a pastel blue. It's silent as a tomb. We pass a series of rooms. I resist the urge to look in. We stop outside Room Fifteen. I step up to the window. Becky is sitting on the bed with her back to me, wearing pajamas with a fuzzy animal motif. Adding a note of cheer. Her hair is pulled back in a tight ponytail, secured with a blue scrunchie. I reach for the knob, the nurse shakes her head.

I tap on the window. "Becky."

My daughter turns around. Her face flashes into a mask of horror. I can hear her scream through the chicken-wire glass.

The big guys each grab an arm. "Let's go," the biggest one says.

Chapter Seven

My apartment is grim and empty. I light a kerosene lamp, the one with the brocade shade. It looks out of place now in my bachelor pad, but my Mom lit it every day of her life. She inherited it from her mother. She called it 'keeping the flame alive.' It's one of the few mementos of her life I've kept, that and her paintings covering my off-white walls.

The visit to Becky at the inpatient clinic is nagging at me. The thought of something happening to her or Jennifer has sent me into a down spiral. Why is Becky so freaked out by seeing me? I look in the bathroom mirror. Nothing's changed, except a little more red around the eyes. Yes, I've been crying, sitting here in this empty apartment in the somber glow of a kerosene lamp. Thinking about the child next in line to keep the family fires burning. What am I doing to keep the flame alive? It's late afternoon. I feel anxious about just doing nothing.

There's someone, or *something*, after me, and my family—been awhile since I thought of them that way. Sitting around worrying is not my usual m.o. I'm more of a guy who wants to wade into the battle. Time to go wading.

I make notes on a pile of cards, cataloging all the inexplicable stuff that's happened since I met Laura Whitcomb; the powder attack, the missing hour, the odd Uber driver. The cards pile up. This makes me feel like I'm doing something, but I sit there staring at them, not making any kind of rational connections. I could be losing my brain, I suppose, but it seems there should be answers on this side of the Twilight Zone.

I uncork a bottle of what George always called 'motivational fluid' and pour a couple of inches in the bottom of a crystal tumbler. My mom left me a set of eight, her favorite vessels for high-brow artist entertainment. She bought them back in the Fifties. Or maybe they were a wedding present.

The taste of Johnnie Walker Green brings back the time when George and I first met. I had just made detective. In the NYPD, partners don't fraternize. Everybody knows that. Especially if one of them is married. We had become friends from the start, laughing, trading insults in true cop fashion. Then one hot August evening, all of that changed. We clocked out and decided to go for a drink. We'd been in a foot chase earlier that afternoon and we were both sweaty. Of course we couldn't go out like that. She invited me to her place down at the edge of China-town, saying she needed to "freshen up."

She came out of the shower wearing a vintage Creedence T-shirt. I tried to ignore her state of half-undress. I don't think she was really trying to seduce me, but I have never been sure. We shared a couple shots of Johnnie Walker Green which she seemed to really appreciate. And then we both realized where things were going. We got as far as her sofa.

We both made a point of keeping our distance around the station, no steamy glances, no furtive touch of the hand. It was obvious we couldn't carry on some torrid affair and still keep our jobs, so we agreed to pretend there was nothing there. And we made that work for the next four years, until I left the force and went off to my private eye career.

—

I saved some case files on my computer from my cop days, though that's against the rules. I don't know if I've been thinking about going back on the force. I doubt they would have me. The file I open is labeled 'The Baka.' The pictures there bring back a night fifteen years ago when my partner, Rick Johnson, and I were on patrol in the Lower East Side. We responded to a call of 'shots fired' and drove into the middle of a firefight raging up and down East Houston Street.

The Baka, the Haitian street gang that had been terrorizing Miami for years, had been trying to carve themselves some new territory out of the Lower East Side.

The gangs already operating there took exception, and the battle was underway. Before our backup could get there, the Haitians riddled our cruiser with bullets. One guy jumped on the hood and fired his AK through our windshield. I took him down, but not before he emptied his clip into Rick's face. I went crazy, grabbed the shotgun and jumped out of the car.

They gave me a medal. I tossed it on the lid of Rick's casket amidst the dirt clods and the flowers. It took a long time to get the hollow sound of it hitting the wood out of my mind. That night comes back to me as I sit there looking at the file. Rick's picture was paper-clipped on the corner of the page. He had been twenty-four. I drain my glass and refill it, deeper this time.

The Haitians were driven out of the Lower East Side and we heard nothing of them for years. But now, according to George, they're back, trying to set up a narcotics trafficking business in New York. Searching online, I find they're still active in Miami. I look at the pictures. Young, tough looking guys with the standard tats, the same 'gonna kill you' expressions I've seen a hundred times on the street. I can't imagine these guys being bossed by a woman—a voodoo priestess. Can't see them hanging women in the park with a perfect hangman's knot. I can see them spraying the crowd with automatic weapons. I did see them do that. No mention anywhere online of the alleged dirtbag, Wilky Mouton, supposedly a member of the gang. Nothing adding up.

I call George, get her machine. "It's Vincent. The Baka. Where are they? What are they doing in New York? Anything specific? Call me."

Shit. Dead ends. It's dark outside now. The East Village hums like the strings of a too-tight guitar. There are probably fifty bars within walking distance of my apartment. I only need one. I throw on my jacket, turn out the lights and head out.

-❧-

The sun finally sets over the East River, fading out the amber halo gilding the taller buildings in Brooklyn. Night had come to the Flatbush neighborhood called Little Haiti. Darkness is deepest across the forested acreage of Greenwood Cemetery. Two transients hiding just inside the cemetery gates slink farther back into the bushes as the gate swings open and a tall, imposing figure in a purple robe walks in.

The woman stands for a moment in the center of a cone of light from a lone streetlight, head swathed in a black scarf. Dreadlocks trail down her back. A handbag hanging over her shoulder immediately draws the two men's attention. The bag is wiggling. Something inside it is alive.

The homeless denizens crouch in the shadows, hold their breaths until the woman disappears into the darkness of the cemetery. They exchange glances, and by mutual agreement, jump up and run out the gate.

Madam Augusta stands in a hidden corner of Greenwood Cemetery before a towering elm tree, kin to the one in Thompkins Square Park where they hung Laura Whitcomb. A sister tree. She feels the spirits gathering around her, as real to her as the trembling leaves of the elm. She holds out her arms, welcoming the ghostly choir.

Her blood stirs as she prepares for the ritual. She sets out three black candles to light the spirit's way, draws sacred symbols on the ground with cornmeal, readies herself for the most important element, the blood sacrifice to the spirits, the *loa*.

She pulls a bone-handled knife from the folds of her robe, blesses the blade with a kiss and reaches into her handbag. The baby alligator squirms in her grasp. The white flesh of its underbelly glows in the candlelight. She avoids the snapping jaws and, with a flip of her wrist, slits the reptile's throat. A fountain of blood erupts, soaking into the earth, nourishing the spirits.

She slips in her ear buds and immediately her head is filled with the sound of drums. She moves her hips in time with the rhythm. The drums grow louder, the tempo faster. She closes her eyes, a beatific smile on her face, dancing with a wild abandon, bare feet kicking up tufts of grass.

The spirit enters her, a primal thrust that sends a jolt through her loins. Sweat pours down her face. At the moment of climax, she summons Gede, the voodoo spirit of sex and death, shouting into the darkness, "Take me, Gede. Take me now."

She falls back onto the grass, body racked by spasmodic jerks. Gebe's voice echoes in her head as she slips into unconsciousness. *"Seize the power!"*

How much time has passed? An hour, two? Madam Augusta opens her eyes, fumbles in her bag for her ringing phone. "Little Jay?"

"Where are you? I've been calling for an hour."

She ignores her son, sits up on the grass, marveling at how good she feels. The spirit is in her, setting every fiber of her being tingling. "Have you found the cop?"

Little Jay explains he has followed the man to an Irish bar at the end of Avenue A. "Kelly's Sports Bar," he says. He gives her the address.

"Stay with him, I'm coming." She disconnects the call, jumps to her feet, and gathers up the artifacts from her ritual. Already the spirits have begun their work. She sings to herself, walking through the darkness of the cemetery. The spirit choir hovers around her, singing harmony.

I stroll down Avenue A toward my favorite Irish Bar. The air is fresh from last night's rain. The storm has moved east, out over the ocean. There must be stars above me, but the city lights wash them out. The darkness is thick underneath the Elm trees in Tompkins Square Park as I pass. The crime scene tape is gone, no trace of the horrific act perpetrated just a day ago. It is sad that life goes on the way it does. Kelly's bar is, as always, warm and welcoming. Hockey is on, as it always is. I find a stool at the end of the bar. It tips as I climb on. Time to dial back the hard stuff. I order a Guinness.

My mood has darkened by the time I finish Guinness number two. Jennifer is still not answering her phone, George likewise. The hospital gives me some nebulous "good as could be expected," bullshit, which is hospitalese for 'fuck off.' My frustration level is rising. Not like me to just sit here in a bar doing nothing. I think of Laura Whitcomb, the look she gave me in Lily's—those green eyes. The touch of her fingers. The stiffness of her body hanging in the shadows of the park. She shouldn't have died. The guy next to me asks for a match, though this is a no-smoking joint. I quit smoking twenty years ago, but I reach in my pocket out of habit, pull out a crumpled piece of paper, the one I took out of Laura Whitcomb's pocket. The guy looks at it and shakes his head.

"I don't smoke." I say. "Sorry." I flatten the paper out on the bar. It advertises an art gallery opening. The address is on Saint Mark's Place, about eight blocks away. The place is probably closed, but it's better than sitting here on my ass getting sloshed—more sloshed. I pay my tab and step out onto Avenue A.

The woman who gets off the Six train at Astor Place stares around the station, as if seeing it for the first time. There's a gleam of excitement in her eyes that the other riders take for urban craziness. But she has had a vision on the subway—a stream of light piercing the rocks far underground. It sizzles and burns. It is the source of the power she seeks. The subway riders give her a wide berth as she climbs up the stairs onto the street, punching numbers into her phone.

"I'm here. Where are you?" Madam Augusta says.

"He's walking along Saint Marks place," Little Jay tells her.

"I'm just around the corner. You've done a wonderful job, my son."

If his mother's ebullient attitude seems strange, Little Jay says nothing. He has seen her possessed before. Best to stay out of the way. "Thanks, Mom." He hangs up.

A few minutes later, she joins her son in an alley off St. Marks Place. He points across the street at a man peering into a shop window. But Madam Augusta is scarcely paying him any attention. The feelings flowing through her now are so powerful she can barely speak. When she does, the sound is deep, guttural. Someone else's voice. "This is the portal. I've seen it in a dream. The source of the power I seek. This man has found it. He's working with the Wiccans. They will learn to heed my warnings." She fishes in her handbag, comes up with a black leather pouch, wrapped with steel wire. The vapor rising from it burns Little Jay's nose. He steps back, manages a weak smile. "Careful with that stuff."

The gallery's name is spelled out in tiny wooden toilet seats above the door: "My Kid Could Do That." The lay person's classic put-down of modern art. This place, toilet seat logo and all, was somehow important to Laura Whitcomb. Right now, it's the only lead I have. My kid could detect that.

A woman inside is arranging a group of sculptures that look, in the dim light, like giant pieces of cake and slabs of pie. I realize she's installing the show advertised in the flyer I found in Laura's pocket. A plaque in the window announces, 'Confection Connections.'

My attention goes to a painting hanging inside on a gallery wall. I'm suddenly transported back twenty years. The savage slanting of paint from the palette knife, the wild arrangement of biomorphic shapes and narrow triangles on a cobalt blue background, is still compelling. From a distance these elements somehow arrange them-selves into a woman's face. It's an amazing work, but I may be prejudiced.

The person installing the show, a cadaverous woman in a Dashiki and a metallic silver head scarf, notices me, shakes her head, a 'we're closed' gesture. I'm still staring at the painting. The woman, perhaps sensing a potential sale, walks over and unlocks the door. A silver pentagram hangs around her neck on a leather thong.

"You look pretty enthralled by that painting," she says. "It's called—"

I finish her sentence. "Self Portrait in Blue."

"Sounds like you know about art."

"I know this work."

She puts on her charm-the-customer face. "Not really representational. The artist was a beautiful lady."

"She was."

"You knew her?"

"She was my mother."

Her smile widens. "Would you like to come in?"

A series of sculptures are scattered around, resting in pools of track lighting. The nearest one is a geometric thing the size of a dish washer. A hand-lettered card declares it: 'Lemon Cake Two.'

The silver-scarf woman leads me over. "It's a rhombic dodecahedron."

"Of course it is. It looks like a cake."

"Yes. Coated with fiberglass resin."

"And this is art?"

"It's art if I say it's art."

"Well said. What happens when it gets moldy?"

"A lot of people ask that. But it's permanently sealed in." She holds out her hand. "Bridgett Bishop."

"Vincent Richards."

"You're Mary Richards's son? An amazing coincidence." I shake her hand. Cold.

"When is the grand opening?" I ask. Making conversation.

"Aiming for tomorrow night, but if Rebecca doesn't show up pretty soon …" She sees my questioning look. "Rebecca Nurse, the artist."

"Rebecca is a nice name, my daughter's name. We call her 'Becky.'"

Bridgett isn't interested in my family news. She plunges on. "She's bringing one more piece down from Yonkers, a wedding cake. Fabulous. It goes there in the window." She glances at her watch, a military-style thing with a green web band. "Almost midnight. Shit. Excuse me." She pulls out her phone.

I mouth the question, "Bathroom?" The universal Private Eye excuse to snoop. She points toward the back. Office furniture fills a little alcove off the gallery. Computer desk, file cabinet, a printer on a little wooden stand, a comfy-looking black leather sofa. A door leads to a storeroom filled with art debris, easels, empty frames, boxes and cartons. A hallway branches off to the left leading to an outside door. Two doors along the way, one of which, I assume, is the bathroom.

To the right is a strange anomaly. A tall, iron-banded oak door that looks like it dates from the Middle Ages is set back into the wall. Probably not the bathroom. The door pull is wrought iron, formed in the shape of an inverted human nose. The previous owner must have been a history buff with a sense of humor. I shrug, put my fingers in the nostrils and tug. Locked.

I find the commode down the hall to the left, step in, wait a moment, then flush the toilet. I start back toward the storeroom—pull up short. The Medieval door is gone, oak planks, iron bands, nose pull and all. The wall is bare, painted museum gray. I blink my eyes, take a breath or two. Seeing things. Have to catch up on my sleep.

Too late to do any more detecting. Bridgett Bishop stands in the office door behind me. "Damn, she's not answering."

I could ask her about the door, but I choose what I think is a more pertinent question. "Do you know Laura Whitcomb?"

Her sales-woman's mask slips a little. "No. Why do you ask?"

I pull out the flyer, turn it over and read her the hand-written note. "'Please come early. We'll all be here. Love, Bridgett.' Did you write that?"

She looks on the verge of panic. "It's time for you to leave." She grabs my arm, steers me toward the door.

"Laura's dead."

That stops her. "No, she isn't. What kind of game are you—"

"I'm sorry."

"Out. Get the hell out of here." She's crying.

I'm starting to sober up. And I've made the connection. Time to regroup. I walk out, pause for a moment to look back at Mom's painting. The price tag: Ninety-three grand. I must have a couple of million bucks hanging on my apartment walls. Where they're going to stay.

A red SUV pulls up to the curb, a thin blonde wearing a fedora climbs out. She opens the hatchback. The compartment is filled with a huge white form which I assume is the long-awaited wedding cake. She wrestles with it. I walk over to help her, but stop when I see a dark object bounce off her hood and slide onto the pavement. Lavender smoke rises up around the SUV's front bumper. I squat down and peek under. A cloth bag sits there, smoking. I want to run but I drop onto my stomach and reach for it.

A knee slams the middle of my back. I find myself face-down on the pavement, arm still stretched out under the car. A woman's voice shouts in my ear. "What the hell are you trying to do?"

"Get back," I holler over my shoulder. "There's a bomb under there."

The knee on my back presses harder. "Bullshit. I'm calling the cops," she says.

I manage to turn my head and get a low-angle view of her butt. Yoga pants. She jabs a button on her phone.

"No need for that," I tell her. "I'm harmless."

"You're too big to be harmless." She listens to her phone for a moment, then says, "The nature of my emergency is that some asshole is trying to steal my car."

I twist around, snatch the phone and turn it off. She jumps to her feet and backs away, a New York-tough expression on her face. Gold artist's smock over the yoga pants. Pentagram on a black velvet choker around her neck. I'm surrounded by Wiccans.

"Give me my goddamn phone."

I flip it open, pop out the battery and toss it back. She draws back her foot, aiming for a crotch shot.

I tense up. "You don't want to do that."

"No, *you* don't want me to do that."

I sit up. She hops out of reach.

I raise my hands in surrender. "A little advice. First. If you're gonna attack, do it, don't talk about it. And second, in spite of what they taught you in women's self-defense school, the balls are the most heavily defended part of a man's body. The trick is to feint for the balls, which he'll go for every time, and then kick him in the face."

"I can't kick that high."

"Assuming your attacker is lying down. And distracted by your yoga pants."

Color rises in her cheeks. "Pig."

"Hey, *you* jumped *me*."

She says, "You're trying to steal my car."

I nod. "By planting a bomb under it. Very common technique."

"Your sarcasm is … Is there really a bomb under there?"

I point to the column of smoke rising from under her hood.

"If this is a pickup routine," she says, "it's the lamest goddamn …"

A dart of flame. Acrid smoke billows up. The front tires melt and go flat. "Get back." I put my arms around her, turn her away from the car. The SUV explodes. I feel the heat on my back. The hood lifts off in slow motion. The concussion knocks us down. Smoke boils around us in an oily cloud.

Rebecca yells, "My fucking cake."

"You mean your fucking car?"

"My cake. I brought it all the way from Yonkers."

The street is filled with gawkers, cars slowing in the street. We stumble to our feet. Rebecca's face is smudged with soot, her hair a tangle. There's a dazed expression on her face. My whole body aches. Bridgett, the gallery owner, motions frantically from the door. I push Rebecca toward her. "Go. Stay away from the windows." The bastard who threw the firebomb is somewhere across the street. I dodge between the stopped cars, searching the crowd. A guy in a wife-beater tee shirt sees me, does a take and sprints away. The blue and white cap makes him easy to follow. He's on foot because his bike is bent up from slamming into the back of my taxi earlier this afternoon. I yell at him stop. He jerks around and his stocking cap falls off. His right ear is missing.

I race after him. He pulls ahead. The booze I've poured down is threatening to reappear. I stop, prop my hands on my knees and concentrate on stabilizing my spinning head. A blur of movement on my left. A hand in a latex glove reaches out, palm upward. A puff of air on my cheek, a burning sensation and then fade to black.

⁂

A dramatic voice: *"This is a time that is not a time. This is a place that is not a place."* Flashes of red, black, and yellow. A silhouette of a hangman's noose swings in the flickering torchlight. A procession of mourners, long shadows stretching before them, pass by, carrying linen-wrapped bundles across their shoulders. Bodies of the dead.

⁂

Sensation comes back gradually. Bright lights above me. A hand on my wrist. The beeping of some medical instrument. Adding up to 'ambulance.' George sits on a bench beside me. She looks concerned.

A woman's off-stage voice which I assume belongs to a paramedic: "He's coming around. We'll need to check for a concussion. I'll give you five minutes, officer."

Good luck giving Georgia Flores a timeline.

George allows a brief smile. "Have a nice nap?"

"What the hell happened?" I try to sit up, the paramedic lays a blue-gloved hand on my chest.

"Patrol spotted you lying on the sidewalk," George says. "They said a woman in a black turban was stomping on your head. A love affair gone wrong?"

"You haven't lost your sense of humor, Lieutenant. How's your love life? Still dating your service plant?"

"The fire in that SUV burned for almost half an hour," she says. "Two firemen collapsed from toxic smoke. Both of them died on the way to the hospital. They were friends of mine."

"Sorry."

"Damped down my sense of humor."

"I was helping this woman unload her SUV," I say. "Somebody threw some kind of incendiary device. It sent up purple smoke."

George writes in her notebook.

I ask, "What happened to the woman in the robe?"

George shrugs. "Faded into the crowd. She throw the device?"

"I'd bet on it."

"You left me a message this afternoon wanting to know about The Baka. We only know what I told you before. Rumors about a Haitian street gang and a voodoo priestess. This would be her?"

"That's the thing. Smoke bombs and public hangings just aren't their style. Remember I tangled with these fuckers fifteen years ago?"

She nods. "You went rogue on them. NYPD gave you a medal."

"Those punks went in for firepower, blood in the streets. They're not likely to let a woman boss them around. Something isn't lining up here."

"Ideas?"

I have some, but telling her would reveal me to be an evidence-withholding dirt bag. I feign dizziness and flop back onto the stretcher.

George flips back a page in her notebook. "The SUV was registered to a Rebecca Nurse. You know her?"

"Doesn't sound like a real name."

"Real enough, address and everything. Witnesses saw you fighting with her just before the car blew up."

We weren't fighting, I was trying to save her ass, but I don't bother to correct George. "I was walking by, saw the smoke, grabbed her."

"Usually, when a person's car catches fire, and the firemen come to put it out, they stick around to talk about it. Any idea what happened to Ms. Nurse?"

I'm tempted to say, "*Went back to the hospital,*" but my head throbs in earnest. The burning sensation on my face reminds me of the powder attack, my second in as many days. These people are beginning to piss me off. I close my eyes, try to relax. My mind is whirling.

The paramedic says, "That's it, officer."

George lays her hand on my shoulder. "Get some rest." She climbs out of the ambulance and it starts to roll. The siren howls its way down St. Mark's Place, blends with the moan of a distant train.

Chapter Eight

I spend the night in Bellevue, but outside a killer headache, I'm not sporting any serious injuries. Scrapes and bruises. My ear looks like a strange purple vegetable. My face is still red from the powder I got last night. Burns like a bastard. This is getting tiresome.

I call Jennifer as I stumble my way along the street toward my apartment. No answer. Next call: A woman with a deep, soothing voice answers at the psychiatric hospital. "There's been no change. She's resting." A more polite rendering of 'Fuck off.' I push on, elbowing my way, New York style, through the crowd. Angry stares, a few push-backs as I bull my way along, taking out my frustrations on the unfeeling crowd along First Avenue.

I end up on Saint Marks Place. The history of this street always gives me a little *frisson* of excitement. Leon Trotsky and W.H. Auden lived here, Andy Warhol ran a night club on this street, a block from The My Kid Could Do That gallery. My head has started to throb again. I sit down in Big Ginger's coffee shop, my favorite caffeine fill-up. Her daughter, Cathy, is clearing tables. The girl has been waitressing since she was twelve. She is now a hot twenty-one, aware of the snugness of her halter top. She waves. "Hey, Detective Vince."

I wave back. "Not anymore, babe."

Cathy's mom, Ginger, scowls her disapproval at my friendly exchange with her daughter. Other customers have learned that messing with the kid could land one's gonads on the grill, metaphorically speaking. Ginger sets a cup in front of me, fills it from a stainless-steel pot. The bandage on my head warrants a questioning eyebrow. "Nice ear."

I smile. "You should see the other guy."

"I know, not a mark on him." She points a finger-gun at me and sashays into the kitchen showing me a vast expanse of spandex. I reach for my phone. It rings before I can pull it out of my pocket.

George says, "We might have a line on your head stomper. I spent the morning with Brooklyn P.D. running down a Haitian woman, local voodoo priestess. Augusta Louventure. That name sound familiar?"

The first name I don't know but the surname I'll never forget. "Rings a bell."

"Her father and her husband were killed in a firefight with the Baka fifteen years ago."

"I'm the one who killed them."

George doesn't respond for a moment. "She looks good for multiple homicides, plus your head stomping.

Of course she had an alibi for last night. Everybody in her neighborhood was at her house for a prayer service. Mob surrounded our ride. On advice of Brooklyn P.D., I beat a strategic retreat, rather than calling SWAT in to pull us out. We may have a line on her posse. Seventh precinct has their eye on a group of Haitians denned up in a dumpy pre-war walkup off Essex. We're watching the whole bunch, but so far nobody's moving."

"A comeback for The Baka?"

"Points for alliteration, but it's not likely. Pretty low-level bunch. Dealing a little on the street. Seventh is keeping an eye on them, waiting for bigger fish, namely your head stomper. We're looking at her for at least five murders: two fire fighters, the three women hanged. You could contribute immeasurably to my closure rate if you started telling me what you know. While you're alive to tell me."

"Noted. You'll keep me in the loop?" I say.

"Sure, we'd like nothing better than to be your very own security force."

"We can share."

"When do we start?"

"Maybe I can fill in some of the missing pieces. I'll keep you posted."

"Sure you will."

"How's your service plant?"

"Stay away from that art gallery." She hangs up.

There are some big pieces missing and it seems like the biggest one centers around the My Kid Could Do That gallery. So far George and the NYPD are in the dark about the gallery's connection with Laura Whitcomb's death. I'm a little in the dark myself so the obvious next stop is the gallery. First, it's time for a little field research.

Jennifer said something about a coven but all I know about witches is the Salem Witch Trials. I key that into my phone. Nineteen people were hanged on a place called Gallows Hill. The first was Bridgett Bishop, followed a month later by Rebecca Nurse. I see where my newfound gallery pals got their names. Twenty-three people murdered in all.

Back in the Sixteen-Hundreds, about the time Peter Stuyvesant bought the land around here from the Dutch West Indies company, a lot of people believed the devil walked among them. Though I met some nasty characters as a cop, it's hard to believe Old Nick himself strolls the East Village. The unknowns are piling up. Something damn strange is going on. So far there's no way to connect all the threads. Time to tug on one of the loose ends. The only character not reflected in the historical comparison is the weird-ass Uber driver.

I call the ride-share service. A few minutes later my Uber pulls up. Sure enough it's the bald guy in the shiny black Audi. Three thousand ride-share drivers in New

York, they always seem to send this guy—or somebody does.

I walk around to the driver's side, knock on the window. Bald guy rolls it down. I smile, reach in and grab him by the collar. Before he can tighten his grip on the wheel I drag him out through the window, spin him around and bend him face down across the fender. "Who the hell are you?"

He grins over his shoulder. I yank his arm up to the breaking point. The grin fades but he says nothing.

"You have a name?" I ask.

"I have many names." His grin widens. He flails and twists like a wild animal, pulls out of my grasp, does a somersault over the hood and runs away down the street. I chase him half a block before he disappears into a subway stop—one like nothing I've ever seen.

The stop is surrounded by a filigreed metal frame, cherubs and gargoyles twisted and green with age, surrounded by a waist-high iron fence. The entrance, designed to resemble a gigantic open mouth, sports a jagged row of teeth. The stairs lead down into darkness. No signs telling where the train goes. I've never seen the likes of this in the East Village, though I've walked these streets for almost thirty years. I take a deep breath and plunge down the stairs.

The light is dim on the platform, the air tinted with the scent of garlic and brimstone. A tarnished metal turnstile bars the entrance. The floor and the walls are matted with shiny green vines.

Men in suits and bowler hats, women in floor-length dresses from another century stand frozen along the platform. Not statues, but real people in suspended animation. Vines encircle their ankles and crawl up their skirts. I step up to a woman, wave my hand in her face. No reaction. I touch her cheek. Cold—a standing corpse.

Uber guy stands a few yards away, grin splitting his face. I grab for him. He hops over the turnstile, dives into the tunnel and disappears.

I yell at him to stop, of course he doesn't so I plow my way through the knee-high vines and jump into the tunnel after him. As I sprint along in the near darkness the temperature rises. A faint bluish glow fills the tunnel. The walls are smooth—polished yellow stone. Then I notice another oddity. No rails. I'm running on hard-packed earth. They must have abandoned this stop a long time ago.

The bald driver cavorts along the tunnel ahead of me. That's the only word to describe his gait. He skips from side to side, jumps up and down like a kid in a playground. He's playing with me. I kick in an extra gear and close the distance between us. The air acquires a scent of jasmine now. A flash of pale green farther down the tunnel. The color of Laura Whitcomb's dress. Is it her? That would be impossible. All of this is impossible.

Uber guy stops to face me, waving his hands, urging me toward him. His grinning rictus reminds me of the master of ceremonies from *Cabaret*. The light fades. Total darkness. I stop in the middle of the tunnel, listening to silence, braced for an attack. I hear a whistle off in the distance, but somehow I doubt there'll be another train along any time soon.

I make it back to the station platform feeling my way along the wall. The silent, empty platform is dark except for the slatted light coming down from a sidewalk vent. The vines and the frozen people are gone. No stairway. No way out. I hear people walking by up on the sidewalk, talking, oblivious to the prisoner below them. I shout up at them, get no answer.

I jog along the tunnel in the near darkness, getting more anxious with every step. The tunnel bends and I can make out an opening in the roof above me. I shout again. Finally, a face peers down. The man wears a dirty bandana around his head, bib overalls. A sanitation worker.

He shouts, "What the hell you doing down there?"

What can I say? I'm chasing an Uber driver? "How do I get out of here?"

The man's shadow disappears, and in a moment a circular shaft of light shoots down a hundred feet along the tunnel. "Utility access," he shouts. "I'll find you a ladder."

I wait in the darkness, looking around me for any trace of the Uber driver. But I am alone in the tunnel, standing on a narrow concrete shelf above the tracks, hand pressed against the smooth yellow walls. Finally, after what seems an eternity, a ladder clanks down and stands on the ledge.

"Not supposed to do this. Don't sue me if you fall and break your ass."

"Last thing on my mind." I climb toward the street. I can make out the uniform cap of an NYPD officer in the hole above me.

I finally make it up to the street. I'm standing on First Avenue where I started. There's no sign of the ancient subway stop. The nearest real one, Astor Place, is seven blocks away.

"You all right?" the cop asks.

"Fine, thanks."

"Drinking a little today?"

I shrug. "Got on the wrong train."

The officer shakes his head, a seen-everything gesture. "That's no shit." He touches the brim of his cap. "Have a nice day."

The Black Audi is gone. There's a scorched spot down the block where it was parked. The subway entrance has disappeared, leaving a bare sidewalk where someone has spray-painted: "Ride the Mole Train!" Gang graffiti maybe.

Nobody else on the street seems to have noticed the weird subway stop. Maybe somebody slipped me some more knockout powder. I have a vision of an entire world lying underground while the East Village goes on about its wonderfully complex life above. But if you came from East Puckerbrush and didn't know there was a New York subway system rumbling under our feet, you'd be surprised by that.

I'm starting to have a sense that there is a different kind of world just outside my consciousness. According to my recent Internet search, this pattern of weirdness, the disruption of the fabric of ordinary life, has happened before, right around the time of the Salem witch trials. So we're looking at a whole other world underground, a mysterious web, a connection to the dark side of our nature. Is this a rendering of good and evil—in capital letters? And what about this Mole Train? Maybe I've somehow been lured into one of its stops. Worlds upon worlds beneath the earth. Speculating on such wild-ass metaphorical bullshit makes my brain hurt. I stumble back toward Big Ginger's café, head still spinning from my underground escapade.

My stool is empty, my coffee cup still on the counter, nearly full. Steam rises from the top. Big Ginger herself stands behind the counter, red hair tied up with a green silk scarf. "There you are."

"Did you just give me a refill?"

"What? You're gone maybe thirty seconds."

Thirty seconds to chase the Uber driver down a subway tunnel, fumble my way back to the vine-covered platform, climb out of the utility tunnel and walk back two blocks to Ginger's? My second time warp of the week. Pretty soon I'll have to accept that impossible things may not be impossible at all.

Ginger brings the pot over. "Thought you were in the can. You want more coffee?"

I wave her off. "I'm good."

She shakes her head. My second head shake of the morning. Not a good sign.

I take out my phone, look up a number. A woman's voice answers, "My Kid Could Do That gallery,"

"Bridgett Bishop, please."

"She's—she's not available. The gallery's closed." The voice sounds familiar.

"Is this Rebecca Nurse?"

"It is. Are you the flaming car man?"

"I'd like to ask you some questions. Can I come over?"

"No way in hell."

"Come on, it's broad daylight. What could possibly go wrong?"

"Famous last words."

"It's important. You're in danger here."

I promise I won't hurt her. She finally agrees and I walk the two blocks, checking over my shoulder, watching window reflections. No tail. The gallery is closed. A drape covers the windows, a security grille fixed across the door.

I rattle the grille, hear footsteps inside. Rebecca pulls back the curtain and peeks out at me. Still wearing her yellow smock and yoga pants. She unlocks the door, raises the grille and lets me in. The giant plastic cakes and pies are still arranged around the floor, each resting in a pool of light. My mother's painting still hangs on the wall.

Am I losing my mind or is there something different about the painting this morning? I squint at it as Mom taught me, and there's no mistaking it. The abstract female face in "Self Portrait" now looks like Laura Whitcomb. If I don't figure things out soon I'll be in Bellevue along with my daughter.

Rebecca locks up, closes the curtain and motions for me to follow her. We wind our way through the cakes and pies back to the office. Desk, work table, art stacked everywhere, piles of boxes. A green and white knit comforter is draped across the black leather sofa I saw before. I reach for the storeroom door, but Rebecca steps in front of me, blocking the way.

"What's back there?"

"Bridgett has a futon back there. She's still sleeping, had a hell of a night last night." She lays a finger across her lips.

"Talk to me," I whisper.

"Bridgett let me sleep out here last night, because I had no way to get home," she says.

Right. Flaming car.

She folds the comforter, invites me to sit down.

She produces a tissue, wipes her eyes, smearing her makeup. "People have been threatening us."

"The people Laura told me about," I say.

"You talked to Laura Whitcomb?"

I tell her the whole story. My meeting with Laura in Miss Lily's, the powder-blowing guy, finding Laura in the park. Rebecca starts crying in earnest, bending over, hands covering her face. I touch her shoulder, she pulls away.

"Laura's body is in the morgue as a Jane Doe," I say. "She had ID identifying her as 'Valarie Park.' That ID is bogus."

"I know it is." Rebecca reaches in her purse, hands me a driver's license: Victoria Park.

"What the hell? Everybody has fake ID? What is going on in this—coven?"

"We started out with thirteen women, all practicing Wiccans."

"Including my wife?"

She nods. "Now there are ten—nine if Laura is dead. All hanged. It's terrible. We all went undercover to protect ourselves." She blows her nose and goes on. "I can't stop thinking about her, lying all alone in a metal drawer. We have to claim her body, give her a decent funeral."

"That might get you in a lot of trouble. You'd be right in the middle of a homicide investigation. Does she have any family who can—"

"I'll tell them I'm her sister, 'Victoria Park'."

George would love that story. Two non-existent sisters. We would all be in jail by sundown.

"Will you go with me?" she says. "I'm afraid. Whoever is killing my sisters is still out there."

Laura Whitcomb tried to hire me to find out who was threatening the coven. It seems reasonable to believe it was the woman stomping on my head last night on St. Marks Place. I now have a dog in this fight.

Rebecca insists we let Bridgett sleep. We'll leave her be for the moment. Rebecca rents a car. We pick it up and head along First Avenue to the morgue.

As we drive, she starts talking. "We've always been persecuted, but the people who threaten us now are over the top. Three of our members were hanged, supposedly to remind us that the Salem trials are still with us. And Laura, who is—was—our High Priestess, became their prime target. But these people are not interested in religious persecution, they're interested in power."

"What kind of power?"

"This delusional woman believes those of us here in the coven have access to some ancient, mythical power source and she wants it. I have no idea what she plans to do with it—whatever it is. She threatened to keep killing us until we turned it over to her. Three women died and we didn't give it to her, so now she's killed Laura."

"What do you know about this mythical power?"

"That's the thing. I don't know what she was talking about, and I told her so. Laura seemed to know something, but she didn't tell us much. She said she would handle it. Even in our circles, she's a mysterious person. Nobody knows much about her, but she's a great leader. Charismatic."

"She ever mention the Mole Train?" I ask.

"She …"

My ringing phone cuts her off. "Richards."

George says, "You make it home OK?"

"No problem. Look I'm a little busy—"

"Get un-busy and haul your butt down to the morgue. We have a problem."

"No problem, I'm three blocks away."

The New York City Mortuary is a faceless four-story glass and steel edifice that reveals nothing of its macabre inner workings. There is always a scattering of official vehicles parked outside, but the Crown Vic with a thistle in the front seat is the one that catches my attention. Lieutenant Georgia Flores service plant has grown. One of its fronds is trying to make a break out the side window.

George leans her well-configured butt against the driver's side door, talking on her phone. She sees me ride by in Rebecca's rental car and waves us over. I jump out and Rebecca goes to find a parking place.

George eyes the departing car. "Your new girlfriend?"

"I hauled my butt down here like you said, so what's the problem?"

"I come down this morning to witness the autopsy, they go to get the body and it's gone."

"How is that possible?" Given my visit to the ancient subway, *anything* might be possible.

"They drew blood samples when they brought her in. Found tetrodotoxin."

"Zombie powder.' I looked it up. Slows your heart rate, makes people believe you're dead."

"They bury you and then dig you up. This is comic book stuff."

"Not if you believe it."

"But in the middle of Manhattan ..."

"It's a Haitian thing. Ring any bells relative to this case?"

"Come on."

"As of now, the morgue is on lockdown. Don't want any more bodies walking off. Security spotted some guy in scrubs running down the hall. Chased him. He got away. Not much description, he wore a surgical mask. But they said he was missing an ear."

That jolts me. Madam Augusta's minion, who ran over me in Tompkins Square Park.

I say, almost to myself, "They have her."

Rebecca walks up behind me while we're talking. "Someone has Bridgett?" she asks.

"No, someone has Laura."

I expect her to freak out, but she does a quick take and smiles. "No, they don't."

She turns and runs. Lieutenant Flores has primal instincts. You run, she chases you. And she runs like the wind. She catches Rebecca in half a block and leads her back in handcuffs. Rebecca struggles against the cuffs. George swats her on the back of the head, showing her who's boss. "Your chauffer, Vince," George says. "Care to introduce us?"

I fumble for a minute with her fake name. Finally remember. "This is Victoria."

Rebecca says, "Victoria Park." I want to slap my forehead.

"Why does that name sound familiar?" George asks.

"Common name," I say.

"Last name on the phony ID we found on our Jane Doe."

"I haven't done anything," Rebecca says, heat rising in her voice.

George says, "Why did you run?"

"The police aren't always so understanding with us."

"Who's 'us'?"

"Wiccans."

"Well, you've certainly given me cause to regret the error of my ways. But I have a hunch as to who you might really be." She pulls out her cell. "This your voice?" She taps a button: *'The nature of my emergency is that some asshole is trying to steal my car.'*

Rebecca looks away. "I thought that at first, but then I realized he was trying to help me."

"Why did you need help?"

"Getting an art piece out of my car."

George turns her laser focus on me. "Tell me if I've got this right. You just happened to be walking along Saint Mark's Place when Madam Augusta decided to firebomb a total stranger's car. Who was trying to drag a giant plastic cake out of her car?"

I shrug. "Civic duty."

She says, "I'm supposed to drag this comedic shit show in front of the Captain, who still likes you for Jane Doe's murder, by the way?" Our eyes lock. "It's way past time for you to give me a straight story." I know that look and I know what's coming. She pulls another pair of handcuffs off her belt. "You have the right …"

"Do I have to ride with your service plant?"

She spins me around and hooks me up in the blink of an eye. "Don't worry, it's in the front. You'll be in back."

CHAPTER NINE

George puts Rebecca and me together in the cruiser's back seat. George is either getting soft, has forgotten procedure, or is trying to trick us into saying something incriminating. Rebecca leans toward me and whispers, "It was not a giant plastic cake, it was an eco-friendly representational acrylic rendering."

I whisper back, "We're in a lot of trouble here. Cop or not, George might be the only one willing to help us. We have to tell her the truth."

"And she has to believe us, which I believe is unlikely."

George and her service plant stare straight ahead but I know she's taking in every word, taping it for all I know. For the benefit of the recorder, I say, "Lieutenant Flores is one of the finest officers ever to grace the NYPD. Her professional ability is outweighed only by her personal charm."

George pulls over into a no-parking zone trying not to laugh. She reaches under the dash and pushes a button. Recorder off. "Damn it, why do I always let you do this to me?"

To Rebecca I say, "See, not all cops are bad."

"Not if you're a white male."

I nudge her, shake my head. "I got this."

George reaches down and turns the recorder back on. "Speak."

In one of those Dirty Harry movies, Harry says, "Man's gotta know his limitations." That's where I am now. Up against my limitations. Madam Augusta has already killed seven people and she's targeted Wiccans for reasons at which I can only guess. My wife is conceivably on her hit list, along with my daughter. And I have no idea how to stop her.

There are several thousand NYPD officers at work in the naked city, and I'm going to need their help. I need George on my side so I have to tell her something, limited to the above ground world she knows and believes in. The dark supernatural underside, she won't buy. I'll have to handle that on my own.

I clear my throat. "Let me be honest with you." The words that almost always precede a lie. George pinches the bridge of her nose, shakes her head.

"You know most of the story," I tell her. "Madam Augusta is trying to set up a drug franchise in the East Village. Some people don't like that. The thing that's missing is Madam Augusta's connection with the art gallery.

"I found a scrap of paper in the café where I met our Jane Doe, whose real name is Laura Whitcomb. A flyer for an art show at a gallery on Saint Marks Place. Stuck it in my pocket, forgot about it. Dug it out later and decided to check it out."

"Found a scrap of paper you forgot about? And Madam Augusta showed up at the same time you were checking out the gallery?" George isn't buying it.

"I don't know, maybe she followed me. Anyway, it turns out a coven of Wiccans has something Madam Augusta wants. And she's threatened to keep killing them until she gets it. Laura was death number four, by hanging."

"Hanging the witches. That has a ring to it. So the Wiccans are based in an art gallery?"

Rebecca shakes her head. "The owner of the gallery is just one of us."

George says. "What does Madam Augusta want?"

"We don't know," Rebecca says.

The answer lies somewhere in the supernatural underground, a place I can't go and still hold onto a shred of credibility with George. I shrug, show I am part of the 'we have no idea' group.

"So Laura Whitcomb," George tries out the name, "wanted to hire you as a bodyguard?"

"Something like that."

George says, "A while ago, Ms.—" she looks down at her notes, "Parks, you indicated that you didn't think Madam Augusta's thugs had Ms. Whitcomb. Why is that?"

"She's gone—somewhere else."

"You telling me she's in God's hands now? Come on. One resurrection is enough."

And again, we dive into the supernatural underworld. "Somebody obviously broke in and stole the body," I say. "How did that happen in a locked-down place like the morgue?"

"I intend to find out what's happening in the real world. We have an APB out for Augusta Louventure and her one-eared functionary. We'll handle them. You stand down. Clear?"

"The Wiccans are still a target."

"That's not a priority right now," George says.

"Of course not," Rebecca says.

I jab her in the ribs. To George, "Maybe we can make a deal—"

Before I can finish, her radio squawks. "*Fifty-One-Fifty, respond ten-twenty-one to dispatch.*" My memory gets a little poke at the use of the radio call sign. It used to be mine. The cop jargon means call the dispatcher by phone. The radio net is not secure.

George puts her cell phone to her ear. "Flores." She listens for a moment "Shit. I'm en route." She puts away her phone, turns to her back-seat prisoners. "They've spotted Madam Augusta down on Essex Street. They're moving in." She pulls us out of the car, unhooks us. She has that hunter's look in her eyes but we are no longer her prey. Nevertheless, she pokes a finger in my chest. "You and I are not done." She jumps in her car and speeds away, code three.

⚫

Little Jay runs up four flights of urine-tinged stairs, rushes into a shabby two-room apartment and throws himself into an overstuffed chair. He tries to get his breath. Sweat soaks through his scrubs.

Madam Augusta comes in carrying a bag of groceries. She stands over him. He cringes, presses himself against the back of the chair. She sets down the bag, reaches out and touches his arm. "I'm not gonna hurt you. Just tell me what happened."

Little Jay's brother, Wilky, slouches in the corner on a dilapidated green sofa, the only other piece of furniture in the apartment. A cushion supports the cast on his foot, a police scanner sits on his lap, ear buds stuffed in his ears. He looks up and says, "Tell her how you fucked up, brother."

"Shut up, fool."

"Tell me," Madam Augusta says.

Little Jay draws a long breath. "I go into the morgue like you said, carrying a clipboard, look like I know where I'm going. An alarm goes off and I thought I was busted.

A couple of the doctors come running down the hall, hollering at each other, freaking out, saying Laura Whitcomb's body was gone. They yelled at me, and I took off running. They almost caught me," he lets a note of pride creep into his voice, "but I was too fast."

"You was too dumb," his brother calls from the sofa.

"I'm comin' over there."

Madam Augusta silences them both with a glance and walks to the window. She gazes out, hands clasped behind her, but her focus is not on the bustling traffic along Essex Street. After a long moment she says, voice subdued, "The body is gone."

"Somebody stole it?"

Madam Augusta shakes her head, stares at her two sons. "This woman is not of this world. She's back from the dead. I know something about that. I need to talk with the spirits. You tell the rest of the guys what's going on. Then shut up and keep your eyes open." She walks into the bedroom and slams the door.

With a sigh of relief at escaping his mother's wrath, Little Jay walks to the apartment next door. This one is larger, a two-bedroom corner unit. Half-a-dozen young Haitian men in various stages of undress are scattered around the living room or sacked out in the bedrooms. They have known each other since they were toddlers and all have come to join Madam Augusta with the promise of big money in the drug trade. They are still loyal, but there is no sign yet of the big money.

A tall man in a tight red satin shirt sits at the kitchen counter eating spaghetti off a paper plate. He lays down his fork and wipes his hands on his pants. "You got us some product, man?"

"Soon," Little Jay says. "Some bad shit just went down. Mama is freaked out."

"More of that voodoo shit?"

"You be careful with that kind of talk. Mama believes it, so you at least gotta make like you do."

Red shirt tosses the paper plate into the sink behind him. "I'm starting to think all this shit is make-believe."

"Listen, any time you want out, you just holler, go back to sellin' your ass on Grand Street."

Red shirt stands up, knocking over his stool, but Little Jay raises a placating hand. "We have to let things cool off for a little while. Chill."

Little Jay walks back to the smaller apartment. Drum-heavy music drifts out of the bedroom, he can hear Madam Augusta chanting. The smell of incense wafts into the living room. Little Jay nods at the bedroom door. "What's she up to in there?"

Wilky is still focused on his police scanner. He pulls out his ear buds. "Séance. Some shit." The two exchange a look, then settle on the sofa. Wilky reinserts his ear buds.

They're not looking at each other now, waiting until it's over.

Finally, the bedroom door bursts open and Madam Augusta stands, arms outstretched, a faraway look in her eyes. A red scarf is draped across her shoulders, garlands of beads around her neck. The guttural voice is back. "I have been given guidance. The spirits have shown me how to enter the portal."

"Mom, are you sure—"

She cuts Little Jay off. "I have seen the portal. I have felt the power."

Wilky jumps up off the sofa, holding the scanner, his cast stuck out ahead of him. "Cops coming." He hobbles to the window and stares down at the police cars pulling up in front of the building. An armored car rumbles down Essex Street. People scatter. He turns. "Mom, we gotta—"

Little Jay and Madam Augusta are gone. Wilky hobbles down the empty hallway calling out his mother's name.

Rebecca and I roll into the psychiatric inpatient clinic in her rental. I've asked her to stop so I can check on Becky. As we stand together in front of the glass-caged reception desk, I realize my mistake. "Is this the child's mother?" the nurse asks.

No use lying. "No, she's a friend."

The receptionist, her face expressionless, checks her schedule board and turns back to me. "I guess nobody told you and your 'friend.' Your daughter was released this morning."

My red face has nothing to do with magic powder. We hustle back to the car, I dial Jennifer's number.

Disconnected.

I'm stunned. I can't believe it. I stare stupidly at my phone. "She's gone. She's taken Becky."

"She has *custody* of Becky," Rebecca says, "and we don't know she's gone." Both reasonable observations, which do nothing to diminish the fear twisting my gut. She's looking at something on her phone.

I say, "I want to go check on her, except I don't know where she lives."

"I do." Rebecca pulls out onto Avenue C. "That's where we're going." The little voice on her phone emits a mechanical chirp: "*In half-a-mile, turn right onto Houston Street.*"

"How is it you know where my wife lives?"

"It's actually her roommate I know about."

"Who would that be?"

"That would be Laura Whitcomb."

That tidbit snaps me into full alert. "You're just telling me this?"

"You don't need to have all our secrets. Their apartment is on Suffolk," Rebecca says. "Essex is a couple of blocks over." The street where NYPD spotted Madam Augusta. The voodoo priestess showing up almost next door is too much of a coincidence. But it may be moot. They've probably rounded her up by now. I call George to make sure. No answer. I leave a message. We double-park in front of a new-looking brick building on Suffolk. Rebecca climbs out. "Keep an eye on the car." A delivery van squeezes by, the driver not amused.

Rebecca stays up in the apartment for fifteen minutes. Twenty. I'm getting antsy. I climb out of the car, Anxious to *do* something. On the street in front of the car someone has scrawled "Ride the Mole Train!" I'd swear it wasn't there when we drove up. I climb back in the car to ponder the situation.

Finally Rebecca slides into the car next to me. "Nobody there," she says. "No sign of a struggle. I did find something, though. I shouldn't show you this, but I guess, since Laura is …" She can't bring herself to say it.

"Laura is *dead*. I'm pretty sure she is."

"Pretty sure? Right. So where's her body now?"

I could swear I caught a glimpse of Laura's green dress down in the other-worldly subway. But I can't answer that question with anything from the 'real world.'

"What did you find up there?" I can hear the impatience in my tone. Stress getting to me.

Rebecca pulls a book out of her purse. It's bound in blue leather, pages edged in gold. "Laura Whitcomb's journal. Wiccans call these 'The Book of Shadows.'" She hands it to me. Inside the front cover, in perfect copperplate: "Love is the fire that turns the earth."

I fan the pages. A yellowed newspaper clipping falls out: Comes now the story of the SS McKinley, a freighter out of Salem, Massachusetts. She went down around three in the afternoon on the 27th of February, 1795, at or near the entrance to New York harbor, just off Staten Island. It was a clear day and the ocean was calm. A fishing boat saw her go down. No explosion, no collision, no fire. She just seemed to be pulled "under by a giant hand." According to witnesses there was "an evil plume of sulfur smoke on the water for an hour afterward."

"Laura's notes say the site is along a ley line that connects to the Thompson Park vortex."

"Ley lines, vortexes. You realize none of that is real?"

"*Something* pulled the SS McKinley under."

"So this power, whatever it is, that sank the McKinley back in seventeen-ninety-five is the power Madam Augusta wants?"

"She's asking for a myth. How can we give her a myth?"

I snap at her, "How about we give her the chair?"

"Relax, Vince. Breathe."

"I don't feel like meditating right now, thank you."

"Try it sometime." She lays her hands on my forehead. Her fingers feel cool. "Your psyche is tied up in knots."

She goes into an explanation of breath-counting meditation.

I'm out of patience for woo-woo. I try to bring us back to reality, whatever that is. "So other than the Book of Shadows, what did you find?" I ask.

"A lot of Jennifer's clothes are gone, her makeup stuff from the bathroom. She just disappeared."

"And took my daughter with her."

"Didn't look like she was coming back any time soon. She knows about Madam Augusta. She must be terribly afraid."

"That's not all she's afraid of." A quizzical look from Rebecca. I tell her the horror story of visiting my daughter in the psychiatric hospital, how she freaked out when she saw me.

"That sounds familiar," she says. "The young girls who accused the women back in Salem three-hundred years ago."

"Only this time, I'm the witch."

"Welcome to the club. You wonder why we all carry fake ID. The witches disappeared a long time ago, but witch hunting didn't."

Chapter Ten

Rebecca and I have taken the rental car back and we're sitting in Big Ginger's cafe. Turns out it's one of Rebecca's favorites as well as mine. The lunch crowd has thinned out. We find an empty booth in the back. Both of us are on edge. I sit facing the front door, my back to the kitchen. Ginger has gone home, leaving her niece, Cathy, to wait on us. She brings us bowls of corn chowder, the house specialty. Rebecca orders a large iced tea, I go for coffee.

Rebecca stares past me at the swinging door into the kitchen, her mind back in another time. "It started in the spring of sixteen-ninety–two," she says. "A group of young girls in Salem, Massachusetts claimed to be possessed by the devil."

"We seem to be following a three-hundred-year old playbook straight out of Salem, Massachusetts," I say. "According to what I read, the 'witches' were accused by young girls driven into a fit by a fungus called 'ergot,' the stuff somebody threw in my face. One of the accusers describes how the devil came to her in a dream with elaborate images of black dogs, red cats and yellow birds, the exact thing I saw in my vision in Lily's on Seventh Avenue. Along with images of people being hanged. So this Salem scenario is repeating itself in the East Village. How can that be?" I ask.

"Laura believed a dark energy field existed back then, and it's still with us," Rebecca says.

I tell her my experience in the magic subway station, the strange Uber driver, the sounds of train whistles that nobody else hears, my oddly prophetic dreams—images that could only be the witch trials.

She nods, like it's quite ordinary. "I can see it in your aura."

"See what?"

"An energy field, like an outline around your body. It's hard to explain. It's getting stronger."

I'll bet it is. I wonder if my daughter saw it, too. "This isn't about me. Tell me about Laura."

"She's a very unusual person. I'm not sure exactly what—or who—she is, but she's not like the rest of us."

I notice her using the present tense. "How so?"

"Nobody knows where she came from. She was your wife's friend. I think maybe they knew each other—earlier."

I don't remember Jennifer mentioning that, but I let it go.

"She has a *presence* about her," Rebecca says. "We all listened to whatever she had to say. She told us there was a kind of psychic energy flowing through us that lies deeper than the physical, and doesn't follow the physical rules of time and space."

The announcer's voice from my dream comes back: *This is a time that is not a time, this is a place that is not a place.* I'm creeping myself out. Maybe I do have an aura.

"This energy has flowed through us since time began. Remember your Greek mythology?"

"Sketchy."

"A character named Daedalus?"

"Father of Icarus, who flew too close to the sun and melted his wings, right?"

"Daedalus built a labyrinth."

"To hide a white bull or something."

"Right. Ovid called it, 'A mazy multitude of winding ways.'" Rebecca thumbs through Laura's journal, points to a page. "She wrote, 'Daedalus never escaped, be careful.'"

"Be careful of a Greek myth?"

"All those stories have endured because there's some central truth in them. This one is about concealing a dangerous power under the ground, out of sight. Laura thinks it still exists, but each generation changes it a bit. As she puts it, 'People see the world by the lights of their age.'"

"And we see it now as some kind of mythical subway running under Manhattan."

"Have you seen the graffiti, 'Ride the Mole Train!'?"

"I thought I was the only one," I say.

"All the Wiccans have seen it, but you're the only one who's been down in a subway station."

My chowder is cold. It was delicious but my appetite has deserted me. A couple in the next booth pay their tab and leave. Cathy is circulating, refilling coffees. She tops mine off, flashes me a smile. Kid has a future in the restaurant business, if she doesn't become a star softball player instead.

I tell Rebecca what I know about Madam Augusta's plans to build a drug empire in New York, and how the odds are stacked against her. "The cartels, the mob, don't have much patience with upstart competition. Maybe she believes she can transport drugs on a magic train."

"She's counting on a myth to save her drug trafficking career?" Rebecca says.

"Aren't we all?"

My phone rings. George is returning my call. "Tell me you got her," I say.

"We have some kind of security breach. Madam Augusta knew we were coming. Apartment was empty. We arrested a bunch of people in the next apartment, one bag of weed between them. The chief is pissed—" A radio squawk in the background. She puts me on hold.

A minute later, she's back. "They spotted her running into the Essex Street Trolley Station."

I know the area from my patrol days in the Seventh Precinct. The city abandoned the station in the late Forties when they stopped using Trolleys. Now it's a maze of tunnels, pitch dark. A labyrinth.

"We sent in two canine units," she says. "The dogs came out with their tails between their legs. Wouldn't go back in. Belgian Malinois don't act that way."

My instinct is to go hunting Madam Augusta, but if the dogs can't find her …

"She's out there somewhere," George says. "Watch your ass. And stay away from Essex Street."

The booths are empty, a few stragglers still sit along the counter. Lunch hour at Ginger's is winding down. Rebecca and I are still deep in conversation. She looks up and points behind me. Her mouth drops open. "Vince, look out."

One-ear boy is rushing toward me, knife upraised. He pushes past Cathy, spilling her coffee. She whips the steel pot at him, a vicious sidearm. It bangs against his forehead, splashes the steaming coffee in his face. He drops the knife, stumbles into the kitchen pawing his eyes, whimpering.

Cathy stares after him. "I didn't want to hurt him."

I put my arm around her shoulder. "You did good, Cathy. Saved my life."

A shy smile. "Aunt Ginger taught me that move."

Rebecca is frozen in place, eyes wide. Her glass has tipped over, trailing tea and melted ice onto the floor. "Call the gallery," I say. I pick up the knife and bust through the swinging door into the kitchen. A man in cook's whites lies face-down on the griddle. A carving fork sticks out of his back. He's not feeling the hot metal cooking his cheek. The rear door stands open. I poke my head out into the alley.

A rumble under the street, the asphalt shifts and I go down, whack my chin on the pavement. A screech— rubber on asphalt. A car careens down the alley, knocks over a row of garbage cans. A black Audi.

The underground rumble gets louder, the asphalt jumps like a carnival ride. The motion pounds my chin on the ground. I struggle to keep my eyes on the fleeing Audi.

The car turns left out of the alley onto Saint Marks place. The My Kid Could Do That gallery is two blocks away. The earthquake, or whatever it was, subsides. I get up and run back through the kitchen, stopping only to pull the cook off the griddle. A patch of his skin stays behind. I pull out my phone and call George. "May have found Madam Augusta," I say.

"Where are you?"

"Big Ginger's cafe. It's on—"

"I know where it is."

"The cook is dead. I spotted a vehicle fleeing the scene."

Her siren screams, and I imagine her, foot to the floor, fire in her eye. "Description?" she asks.

"Black Audi."

"Get a license?"

"Plate covered with mud."

"The ride share that picked up you and your wife?"

"Afraid so. Can you send a car to the My Kid Could Do That gallery?"

"Why?"

"Pretty sure that's where the black Audi is headed."

"That where Madam Augusta is?"

"I don't know, but she's close. I can feel it."

"Feel it? Great. Thanks, witch-boy." She disconnects the call.

I dash back inside. Rebecca is cursing at her phone. "Pick up, pick up, dammit." Bridgett is not answering her phone.

"Stay here," I say. I open the front door of the café. George's unmarked pulls up. I run down the street toward the gallery. George chases me, shouting something I can't quite understand. I glance over my shoulder. Rebecca has joined the procession. A blue and white pulls up, patrol officers race into Big Ginger's.

Our procession covers the two blocks to the gallery in record time. George passes me. The woman can run. She wants Madam Augusta bad—at least as much as I do. A crowd gathers, drawn by the sirens. She shouts, "Get back," eases the front door open and noses into the gallery, gun first. No waiting for backup. Vintage Flores.

In a moment, she shouts, "Clear."

I step in, careful to stay out of her line of fire. The gallery is empty, the giant plastic cakes and pies undisturbed. I follow George into the office. She motions me back, advances down the hallway. Bridgett's metallic silver scarf lies crumpled on the floor. The back door is knocked flat, ripped off its hinges. George holsters her Glock. "Shit."

Rebecca is crying. "I love her." I put an arm around her shoulder, whisper reassurances about getting Bridgett back. Uniforms have stretched yellow tape securing the crime scene. George doesn't seem sympathetic to Rebecca's feelings. "Is there a security camera here?"

Rebecca nods, and in a moment we're watching a tiny black-and-white monitor. A lot of nothing for several minutes, then Bridgett walks out of the office and inspects the giant cakes and pies, wiping some non-existent dust off Lemon Cake Number Two. A man rushes out of the back. Dreadlocks, tank top, big muscles. He grabs Bridgett. She fights back, rakes her fingernails down his face, aims a knee at his groin. He punches her in the face and she goes limp. He throws her over his shoulder like a sack of wheat. She was a handful for one guy. I would bet the one-eared guy was supposed to be part of this raiding party, until Cathy clocked him with her coffee pot.

The office door swings shut, then pops back open. Another figure appears. Bald head, wispy mustache. Our Uber driver smiles at the camera.

"Piece of shit wanted us to see him." George says.

I remembered his mocking little dance in the phantom subway. "Safe bet."

George is getting steamed. "Who is he?"

I have an idea, but it is so preposterous I decide to keep it to myself and answer her with a shrug.

"Any other cameras?"

Rebecca shakes her head.

George points to the recorder. "I'll need that disc." She walks out among the cakes and pies, talking on her phone. A few minutes later three more cruisers roll up. The rest of the cavalry has arrived, but they're too late. This was an all-out assault. Abduct Bridgett, kill me. We're dealing with somebody half-a-click left of sanity. I hope that somebody isn't me.

Madam Augusta has a hostage and has two ways to go: demand the password, or the incantation, or whatever the hell it is, in exchange for Bridgett's return, or torture the information out of Bridgett. The only problem is, Laura Whitcomb is the only one who might possibly know how to get on the Mole Train, and she's dead.

Rebecca sits on a gallery bench, head in her hands. The wall behind her is empty. My mother's painting is gone, frame and all. I wonder if it still bears the likeness of Laura Whitcomb. I can't resist a peek back in the storeroom. The big oak door with the upside-down iron nose is still gone. If it was ever there.

CHAPTER ELEVEN

The gallery phone rings. Rebecca picks it up. "My Kid—" Before she can get the name out, the caller cuts in. I can't make what the tinny voice is saying, but Rebecca's expression makes the purpose clear: This is our ransom call.

I motion to George. She figures it out in a second and is on her phone trying to set up a trace. Rebecca says, "We don't *know* ... You must be crazy." An outburst from the caller. I shake my head—careful with the crazy talk. Rebecca nods her understanding and says, "Can you please just bring her back? We won't hurt you." She's not speaking for all of us, but I let that slide.

George gestures to Rebecca, rolls her hand. Keep her talking.

Rebecca tries to explain to the caller that the Mole Train is a myth, "Not something you can throw your bags on and ride to Cleveland." Apparently, her sarcastic tone goes down poorly. She shouts at the dead phone. "We'll get you, fucker!"

George puts down her phone, smiles. "They got the trace. About six blocks away, Lower East side." She is out the door, heading for her car. I keep pace with her this time, hop in her unmarked, pulling in my knees to avoid her service thistle. Damn thing has grown. A couple of leaves creep toward the windshield now.

*

We head down Avenue A toward Essex. Traffic is heavy. Seventh Precinct units are responding and will probably beat us there. That pisses George off. She wants this collar. She flips on the siren, pounds on the dash, shouting out the window at slow movers. Finally, she puts two wheels up on the curb and careens along the sidewalk for half-a-block, disregarding the well-being of her thistle.

The trace identified a spot on Delancey near the defunct trolley station where Madam Augusta was last seen. We hit Delancey and George slides to a stop behind a couple of Seventh Precinct cruisers. Four officers are crouched behind their cars, guns drawn. A crowd has gathered. This time there really is nothing to see. It doesn't take long to figure out that Madam Augusta has returned underground. Where the K-9 units won't go.

George sags back in her seat, kills her light bar and lets out an uncharacteristic sigh. "She's a fucking mole."

The irony of the term is lost on George, who's still firmly anchored in the 'real world.' It's time to change that. "A few things I need to tell you." Her eyes blaze. I'm dreading this, but I plunge in. "I don't pretend to know what all is going on, but here's what I know." I run the whole story by her, inexplicable supernatural bits and all.

She sits stunned for a moment, then says, "There's something different about you. Maybe that magic dust messed with your mind. I think you actually believe this stuff."

"Telling you what I saw."

"Fine. Here's what we're gonna do. We're not gonna cast a spell on her, we're gonna send SWAT down there with tear gas and flame throwers and we're gonna blast her out. Good old-fashioned police work."

"Good old violent over-reaction."

"Over-reaction? Are you kidding? She's responsible for half-a-dozen murders. A kidnapping. What do you want me to do, bake her a cake?"

"I might be able to draw her out. I know what she wants, I just have to convince her I can give it to her."

She starts the car, backs across the street. "If you've got a plan, let's hear it."

One is forming in my mind. The more I think about it, the worse it sounds.

"Give me a chance to flush her out. If it doesn't work, then give it hell."

"Your plan?"

"A little time is all I'm asking."

"You're asking me to risk my shield here. If you don't come up with something …" She lets it hang there, but her meaning is clear.

I stop thinking about my crazy plan because there on the sidewalk, in the spot George's cruiser just vacated: "Ride The Mole Train!" Red paint this time. Same insistent exclamation point.

George drops me off back at the gallery. "Get some help, Vince. When this is over."

Good idea, but I'm not sure what kind of help I need, or who the hell might provide it—or when this will be over. The Mole Train has brought old school madness to the Upper East Side. I'm on my own this time.

The My Kid Could Do That gallery is a crime scene. Evidence techs are at work inside, Rebecca is out front on the sidewalk. I bring her up to date on the search for Madam Augusta.

"She called me again on Bridgett's phone," Rebecca says. "She didn't say anything, just let me listen to Bridgett scream in the background. Then she hung up. I wanted to call her back, but I didn't know what I could say that wouldn't make things worse."

I tell her about my plan. Her mouth drops open but she hears me out. Finally, she agrees. We hail a cab and head for The Enchantress to meet the nine remaining members of the coven sequestered there. On the way,

Rebecca gives me a crash course in the coven's brand of occult. "We practice Dianic Wicca. It's a feminist tradition, a social awareness of oppression and injustice experienced by women. You might say we're social justice warriors."

I nod my head, trying to keep my face expressionless. They're not going to like my plan, but it's all I have. She tells me the business about witches casting evil spells on people is bullshit. "Black magic spells are just part of the false mythology around Wiccans. The same bullshit that circulates about voodoo. We're mostly into living in harmony with nature. We're connected to the power of Diana. I believe the Mole Train somehow represents that power."

My head spins. Good power—bad power. But any fantasy I might have held about the Wiccans turning Madam Augusta into a toad is just that. Best not mention it to Rebecca. As we walk through The Enchantress, past displays of Wiccan paraphernalia, and climb the stairs to the upper room where the coven has gathered, I prepare myself for an attack on charges of 'being male.' I vow to suspend disbelief and check my negative attitude at the door.

Rebecca asks me to wait outside. Apparently rituals are closed affairs. I hear voices through the door. Low, chanting, the sound of a flute. I imagine candles and feathers and incense, stuff I've seen displayed on the store's shelves below.

All I hope for is some word of Jennifer and Becky, that they're still alive and haven't fallen prey to Madam Augusta's insane ambitions. My wife never said anything about the Mole Train, but there are probably a lot of things she hasn't told me.

Rebecca ushers me in. The light is dim, the windows draped with rainbow-hued cloths. The smell of incense is overpowering. On the far side of the room is a table draped with an embroidered shawl. It contains objects representing the four magical elements: Incense burner for Air, a bowl of water for Water, a red candle for Fire and a bowl of salt for Earth, Rebecca told me. An alter, maybe

The seven remaining Wiccans stand in a circle. Four of the original thirteen are dead, hanged in public places in the East Village. Also missing are Bridgett, now in the hands of Madam Augusta, and Jennifer, in God's hands for all I know. The women's expressions are grim. The looks I get are not welcoming. My plan is going to be a hard sell. Rebecca, my only ally, smiles at me and gestures for me to speak.

Public Speaking was my most hated high school class. "I know you don't trust the police, but believe me, they're doing all they can." I estimate the Wiccans' faith level for that assurance is zero. Can't fault them for that. My own motto has always been, 'never believe anyone who says, "believe me."'

I explain that Madam Augusta has taken Bridgett underground to a defunct trolley station. The police are planning to send SWAT in after her. I see from their expressions that this does not inspire confidence—probably images of tear gas, automatic weapons and a lot of blood. "It's dangerous, but it's the only thing they can do." I hope George was kidding about the flame throwers.

"You expect us to trust these people?" a short brunette asks. "All we ever get from them is harassment."

"Look, my wife is part of this—coven. And for all I know Madam Augusta has her ... and my daughter. I have a dog in this fight, whether you like it or not."

The folksy, Lyndon Johnson line doesn't go down well. Mutterings around the room.

Rebecca bails me out. "How can you help us?"

"Well, here it is. I want to become your high priest."

I let the wave of protests crest and fall. Then I tell them what I have in mind. Tell them I think it's our best chance to stop Madam Augusta, and save their lives. "If I understand your tradition, Wiccans gather and direct energies. A high priestess—or priest—focuses that energy. And I know it sounds crazy to let a man be a priest, even temporarily, of a feminist coven, but can you just see me as a human being? One who desperately wants to see his wife and daughter again?"

We sit cross-legged in a circle. No one has offered to sing, *"Kumbaya,"* for which I am grateful. We spend an hour in debate prep. My butt gets tired. The women seem a lot more comfortable in this position than I am.

Rebecca fills me in on what she knows of Haitian voodoo beliefs and rituals. Then it's my turn. "I'm starting with the assumption that Madam Augusta is not playing with a full deck." That brings a nervous round of chuckles. "That's not to detract from her power and influence, but she's up against some pretty stiff, and dangerous, competition trying to sell drugs in the East Village. Her plan was crazy to begin with."

I explain what I've gotten from George and the NYPD about Madam Augusta's fledgling drug operation, and how their raid on her house in Flatbush turned up nothing. "The mob approached me wanting information as to her whereabouts. According to NYPD, the cartels have her on their radar, too. It seems like she knows how to hide from both the good guys and the bad guys." A woman in a red and green dress says, "How ugly is this …"

"Right. The cops have tried to infiltrate her organization, but it's mostly her relatives, people who've known each other all their lives, so that hasn't worked so far. She's under pressure from all sides, and she's desperate. She believes you folks are her last hope."

The group is doubtful of my ability to pull off the Wiccan priest con. "Bridgett's life is on the line here," Rebecca says. "They're torturing her. I can't think about that." She addresses the women in the Wiccan circle. "We have to do *something.*"

They talk among themselves. Finally, there is a mumbling of assent. A thin blonde in a black pants suit says, "Make the call."

My palms are sweating. I've programmed Bridgett's number into my phone. I wipe the screen on my pants leg, take a deep breath and push the button.

"Madam Augusta, this is Thelbow. I am the high priest of the Wiccans."

"Bullshit. I never heard of you."

She's got that right, but I push on, talking in a deep, authoritative radio voice that I imagine a high priest might have. "But I have heard a lot about you. I have been in touch with Papa Legba." This brings a gasp from Madam Augusta. Papa Legba is the intermediary between the gods and humans in the voodoo tradition. She doesn't know I first heard the name in an Elton John song back in nineteen-eighty-two. The gasp tells me she might be buying the scam. "He is not pleased with you," I say.

"What do you want?"

"I have something you want. You have something I want. Let's make a deal." I sound like a cross between

Monty Hall and that New York real estate mogul. The women around me roll their eyes and shake their heads.

Silence on the other end of the line. I can hear voices in the background. She is relaying my message. Finally she says, "Let's hear it."

"What you seek lies in Vilokan." The traditional home of the Voodoo dead, if Rebecca is right. "You are banned by the gods. That is why you have failed."

"I will not *fail*." There is silence after that outburst, then: "What do you want?" Her tone is subdued. I've got my foot in the door.

"You know what I want. The woman from the gallery. She is one of my people. She knows nothing, she can't help you. Bring her back and I will give you the key to what you seek. I know your plans aren't working. You have no way to get product. You are surrounded by your enemies. You are no longer a Mambo, you're a rat, hiding in a hole."

This brings an explosion of vitriol in what I guess is Creole. She switches back to English. "You know a hell of a lot about my business, but you know nothing about the spirit world." The anger is back in her voice.

"Augusta, you tried to kill my immortal priestess. A foolish mistake. Do not make another one. My eyes see into your soul." I'm getting into this improv. Rebecca shakes her head, frowning. Don't overdo it.

"You hide in a tunnel," I tell Augusta, "but you are nowhere near the train you seek."

"I have ridden that train—in a vision."

"So have I, but my ride was no vision." Not entirely bullshit. I've seen one of its stops. If it has stops. If it exists. I plunge ahead. "You can travel anywhere on this train. Columbia, Mexico." Good pickup spots for dope, in case she fails to get the message.

I let the silence hang on the line before I go on. "So, what do you say? Bring my gallery woman to the portal and I will show you the way in." The way into the federal pen, if it works out. The Wiccans are restless. They don't like the expression, 'my gallery woman.' But hey, I'm the high priest here.

"How do I know I can trust you?" Madam Augusta says. A con artist talking about trust.

"I swear by the sword of Vaatu." I almost choke on that one. An imaginary god from a cheesy-assed sci-fi novel.

Surprisingly, she buys it. Tonight she will bring Bridgett to Tompkins Square Park, which, I assure her, is the location of the portal to the Mole Train. She hands over Bridgett, I usher the Madam into the portal. We agree on a time, midnight, of course. Just the two of us. Alone in the dark woods. What could possibly go wrong?

Now we have half a plan—or a half-assed plan, and we have six hours to put the other half together.

Chapter Twelve

A streetlight casts a pool of light on the sidewalk underneath the tree where Laura Whitcomb was hanged. The orange-amber glow reflects off an oversized cross hanging around my neck. My face is hidden by a red leather mask. A black cowl flowing into an ankle-length robe completes my ensemble.

The midnight hour. The high priest has arrived. The priest, realizing he is backlit by the streetlight, feels very much like a target. I am without backup. The Wiccans vetoed telling the police. Rebecca dropped me off, leaving me to disappear into the shadowy woods of Thompson Square Park. The last time I met Madam Augusta, she drugged me and stomped on my head. Maybe she'll bring a gun this time.

A minute past midnight. A voice out of the darkness: "Are you alone?"

I raise my arms in a priest-like gesture. "Each of us in this world is alone." I hold out my arms. "You may approach."

A form, dressed in black, steps from behind a tree. It's the one-eared guy who ran from Laura Whitcomb's hanging. I wonder if he feels weird returning to the scene of his crime. Bridgett, the gallery owner, stands beside him, hands bound, head bowed. Madam Augusta calls out from the shadows, "Here is your woman. It's time to deliver on your promise."

"When you approach the portal, you must deliver an incantation."

"This is not the portal."

"The portal is a place that is not a place," I say.

"The incantation—give it to me."

"Come closer and listen." I slip my hand under my robe, close my fingers around the butt of my Beretta, waiting for her to show her face. Not sure if I could shoot a woman in cold blood, but she doesn't know that. Bridgett stumbles along, half-dragged by the one-eared guy, Augusta's son, her face twisted in pain.

I feel the heat rise in me. "Let her go." It comes out louder than I intended. Her son lets go of Bridgett's arm. She shuffles toward me. I pull out the Beretta, keep it hidden in the folds of my robe.

Madam Augusta steps out of the shadows. The air takes on a chill and a cold fog drifts around us. She stares over my shoulder, her face a frozen rictus. She turns and bolts into the darkness. Before I can turn around to see what's spooked her, one-ear is on me, a knife in his hand.

I block his thrust with my left hand. A sudden blaze of light fills the park. The roar of steel on steel pounds in my head. I bring up the Beretta and fire. I feel the recoil but the weapon makes no sound. I watch his body fall. Bridgett screams and drops into a fetal crouch on the sidewalk. The roar and the piercing light fade.

I pull off my mask and do a quick three-sixty, Beretta held out in front of me. A red light recedes into the darkness, looking for all the world like a lantern hanging on the caboose of a train. The fog dissipates as quickly as it arrived. Not a living soul in the streetlight's glow. I put away the gun, call Rebecca. "Seventh Street gate. I've got Bridgett." Without waiting for her answer, I scoop Bridgett up and carry her out of the park.

The scene is branded on Madam Augusta's brain. From the darkness of the trees she watched her brave son attack the priest, saw a blinding flash of light, heard the roar of a pistol, saw her son fall. The apparition hovering behind the priest—the woman who disappeared from the morgue—was gone. Had she only imagined the vision? Augusta curses herself for her headlong flight in panic. But this is a powerful spirit, returned from the dead. It suddenly occurs to her that if anyone knows the secret of the Mole Train it is Laura Whitcomb. It will take strong magic to overcome her.

All these thoughts flit through her mind in an instant, replaced by an image that remains burned into her brain: The 'priest' threw back his hood and pulled off his mask, revealing Vince Richards, the man who killed her husband and her father—and now her son.

She crouches in the shadows, trembling with rage. He has made a fool of her, pretending to have the key to the Mole Train. Pretending to be a *priest*. Blasphemy. Sins that cannot go unpunished. She runs from the park, face burning with shame, dashes out onto Avenue B and jumps into a waiting car: A black Audi.

We lay Bridgett in the back seat of Rebecca's car. She cradles Bridgett's head as if she were a child, gives her a gentle kiss on the forehead and brushes a smear of blood from her cheek. Her tears fall onto Bridgett's scarf, giving it a deeper, somber tone. This must be what true love looks like. I stand on the curb watching them drive away toward Mt. Sinai up on Seventeenth. As they turn the corner and disappear, George's Crown Vic slides to the curb, light bar flashing.

I climb into the front seat, knees brushing the thistle hanging on the dash.

George says, "Like the robe."

"I shot a guy in the park. Madam Augusta's son."

"Where's Madam Augusta?"

"Got away."

I know she's biting her tongue. She jumps out of the car. "Show me."

The tree where Laura was hanged, where I shot Little Jay, Madam's son, is a hundred yards inside the park. The streetlight still stands sentry in the early morning darkness. Three walkways lead off into the darkness. We circle the plaza, walk around the hanging tree. Little Jay's body is gone.

"You shot the guy right here?"

"Two rounds from less than five feet away."

"Even you …" George shines her mag light on the concrete. My spent brass shines in its beam.

"… couldn't have missed."

She kneels down, moves her flashlight beam across the sidewalk. "Didn't bleed much," she says. "Not at all, in fact." She sighs, a long-suffering expression on her face. "Let me see your piece." I hand her the Beretta. She sniffs the barrel, checks the magazine. "Two rounds missing." She keeps the gun. "Run me through it."

I decide not to argue. She keeps her face expressionless as I outline my plan to pose as the high priest, my disguise, the robe, the cross, the red leather mask, which I hand her. She holds it up to her face, perhaps to hide her smile.

"Madam bought it?" she asks.

"She brought the gallery owner back. I drew my weapon, advanced toward the subject." I have reverted to cop-speak "The subject saw something behind me. She panicked and ran."

"Saw what?"

"Don't know. At that moment, Little Jay comes at me with a knife. I shot him—think I shot him. Actually, I didn't hear the gun go off, but I felt the recoil." I tell her about the beam of light, the roaring freight train noise.

She shines her light in my eyes. "So just as you decide to shoot, a train roars through Thompson Square Park? You'll have to pardon the shit out of me, but I think you're seeing things other people don't see. Maybe we ought to transport your ass down to Bellevue."

"Madam Augusta saw it."

"I don't have time to stand around arguing about imaginary trains. We have a suspect at large here who's killed seven people. Against my better judgment, I made the career-limiting decision to give you time to try out your so-called plan. Now it's time for you to stand down and let the adults to do a little police work." We walk back to her cruiser in silence.

We sit in the cruiser as George works her phone. My mind is filled with memories of our old times together. I keep them to myself. It's almost dawn when she finally hangs up and fills me in on the cops' progress: A forensic team spent the night scouring Tompkins Square Park and came up with nothing. They searched the Lower East Side, probing the old trolley station with similar results. Madam Augusta disappeared back into her hole. They're going to try sonar and infrared next. George repeats her admonition to stay out of police business, kicks me out of her car and drives away, leaving me to walk home alone.

I'd seen a poster somewhere for a Wiccan Street Faire, but I hadn't paid it much attention. Now as I walk across the East Village toward my apartment just before dawn, I find myself in the middle of it. They've blocked off Ninth and Tenth near the park and the street is filled with people in strange costumes which I take to be nymphs, satyrs, pixies and various other pagan denizens. Though the sun isn't quite all the way up, they've already put up tents and booths on both sides of the street, vans are parked alongside unloading boxes of magical merchandise. Eerie flute music drifts over the East Village. A belly dancer floats along, holding up her veil to keep it out of the gutter.

"Blessed be," she whispers.

Dressed as a Wiccan priest, I feel compelled to respond in character, whatever the hell that is. "You got it," I say. She twirls away down the street.

I'm almost home when Rebecca calls from the hospital to tell me Bridgett is sedated and resting well, and will probably recover. They're talking about physically. I doubt that she'll ever get her ordeal out of her head. Madam Augusta pulled out her thumbnails.

The sun is rising as I get upstairs, pull off my priest robes and flop down across my bed. I lay my cell on the nightstand, and then remember I still have Bridgett's number in my phone. Unlikely that Madam Augusta still has the phone, but it's worth a try.

Four rings, then voicemail: "You've reached the My Kid Could Do That gallery …" Bridgett's recording asks me to leave a message. I disconnect the call and close my eyes and let the darkness sweep over me.

I've been asleep less than an hour when my phone rings. Madam Augusta's voice brings me instantly awake. Her voice is oddly robotic, as if she were in a trance. "You kill my family."

"Your son came at me with a knife."

"Next time he will not fail." Next time? I fired two rounds into Little Jay's chest. How could he not be dead? "You killed my husband and my father," she says. "You probably don't even remember."

She is wrong there. I still had nightmares about the firefight with the Baca gang. Seven of the gang died that night, along with my partner. I lost my head when my partner went down, pulled the shotgun from the rack and emptied it at the advancing gang members. I kept firing even after the last one went down. Another cop finally yanked the gun out of my hand. I was on medical leave for a month until I got myself under control. I threw away the pills they gave me and went back to work. They gave me a medal.

The dreams started coming then, surreal images of bloody faces and blind eyes. Jennifer begged me to tell her what was wrong, but I could never find the words. I closed her out until she couldn't take it anymore.

"I have your family now," Madam Augusta says in that robotic voice. Shouts in the background. She muffles the phone. I hear sounds of a struggle, then my daughter's voice, small, tentative: "Hello?"

"Becky, are you okay, baby? Is Mom there?"

A frightened whisper: "*Who is this?*"

"It's your dad, honey. Don't you recognize—"

"We're down here in—" More struggles, a grunt of pain, then silence.

I'm grinding my teeth, my hand sweaty on the phone.

Madam Augusta is back. "She's a pretty girl."

I remember my hostage negotiation training. You trade threat for threat and pretty soon, somebody dies. It's a struggle to keep my voice under control. "What do you want?"

"I want the woman who was in the park last night—"

"What woman?"

"No time for games. The woman who was hanged. She was standing right behind you."

That explains the look of horror on Madame Augusta's face. It didn't, however, explain the headlight and noise of the train.

"This woman has come back from the dead. She's from the spirit world," Augusta says. "She holds the secret to the Mole Train. If you convince her to give it to me, I will return your wife and your daughter."

It takes a second for that to sink in. Two things are clear: Madam Augusta is lying through her teeth. She's intent on getting revenge. No way is she willing to let our little happy little family ride off into the sunset. That has double cross written all over it. The second thing, she is scared to death of Laura Whitcomb. This is a card I might be able to play, except for one thing. Laura Whitcomb is dead, and my connections to the spirit world are pretty damned limited.

Only one course: Go along with her for now, try to figure something out. Something that will keep Jennifer and Becky alive. I tell Madam Augusta that I'll talk to Laura Whitcomb and call her back at noon. Playing for time. Six hours to figure something out.

My first thought is to call George, but if Madam shows up and runs into SWAT, my wife and daughter will likely die in the crossfire. I could turn myself over to Madam Augusta, but that is no guarantee Madam Augusta would turn my family loose after she kills me. Especially when she finds out Laura Whitcomb is not going to give her keys to the mythical Mole Train.

There's no chance of going back to sleep. I keep hearing Becky's frightened little voice. I wander out into the kitchen in my underwear, boil water for the French press and pour myself a mug. My stomach is twisted into a knot, my eyes are burning from lack of sleep, and not a few tears wet my cheeks. I'm at the end of my rope. My last act will be to wade into Madam Augusta's thugs with guns blazing the way I did down in the Lower East Side seven years ago. Maybe this time they'll give me a medal posthumously.

I carry my coffee into the living room. The sun is peeking over the buildings along Twelfth Street. I sit on the sofa, eyes closed, basking in the warmth. My eyelids finally get heavy. I set my cup on the floor and give in to sleep.

Chapter Thirteen

A voice whispers in my ear, "Wake up, Vincent."

I sit up on the sofa, knock over my coffee. My eyes are drawn to a painting hanging over my mantle—one that wasn't there before. The 'Self Portrait' my mother painted is now a shimmering hologram of Laura Whitcomb's face. She's staring at me. "Do you know why I'm here, Vince?"

She still wears her green dress, the white scarf around her neck. What do you say to a ghost? I mumble something, but she cuts me off.

"I'm here, Vincent, because you see things others don't see, and hear things others don't hear."

"I see your face. How is that possible?"

"Because someone else saw the painting this way. The artist who painted it."

"I don't see how that's possible. My mother died before any of this craziness started."

Laura smiles. "So did I."

"Good point."

"Why did your mother name you 'Vincent'?"

"After her favorite artist."

"Poets say Van Gogh saw the nails that attach the colors to things and he saw that the nails were in pain. He, too, saw connections no one else could see. Your daughter screamed the last time she saw you. What do you think she saw that others could not?"

I wonder about that. But I'm afraid to hear the answer. Is there some demon inside me? I remember her voice on the phone: *Who is this?*

Laura says, "A powerful ribbon of mystery connects us across the ages. A blessing or a curse, depending what you make of it. You are part of that ribbon."

"Is this where the train comes in? You know, I haven't ever really seen the train. I guess I'll believe it when I see it."

"No, you'll see it when you believe it," she says.

"Madam Augusta thinks her life depends on getting on the train."

"It does, but in a way she might not expect. She doesn't know it only travels in one direction."

I'm pretty sure I know what direction that is. The coffee puddle on my floor is spreading toward my bare foot. I try to wipe it away with my hand, touch my bare leg. I realize I'm sitting there in my skivvies talking to a ghost. "You'll have to excuse me."

"Go get your pants on, and make some more coffee. I could use a cup."

"You drink coffee?"

"Tea is a little weak for my taste."

I jump up and head for the bedroom. Her eyes, of course, follow me in my tighty-whities. I feel heat rise on my neck.

I dress, hurry back to the kitchen, fill the kettle. Laura watches me. I say, "Can you see—everything?"

"Only what I need to," she says. The water boils, I pour it into the French Press. While it steeps, I walk back into the living room. Glance up at Laura's image in the picture frame above the mantle. The mantle scene is reflected in my glass table. In the reflection the picture frame is an empty black square.

I do a double take, look up at the mantle. Laura smiles at me. I'm getting used to seeing things I can't understand. "I assume you showed up to save me in the park last night."

"In spite of your many faults, you're on the side of the angels. Fighting above your weight here, however."

I pour two mugs of coffee, set them out on the counter. "What many faults?"

Laura stares at me from her perch on the mantle. The coffee recedes in one of the mugs. "Not bad," she says. "Got any sugar?"

This is the oddest breakfast I've ever had. I pour in two packets of sugar. "You probably know Madam Augusta has my family." I explain Augusta's demands: Access to the Mole Train in exchange for the safe return of my wife and daughter. "Probably a trap. I killed her husband and her father. She wants me dead."

A sardonic smile plays on her lips. Her gaze turns to steel. The wooden frame around her smolders. A curl of smoke rises toward the ceiling. A smoke alarm screeches. Laura throws it a glance. It stops.

"Madam Augusta is scared of you," I say. At this moment, so am I.

"She's wise."

"It's eight o'clock. I have four hours to get back to Madam Augusta. What shall I tell her?"

"Tell her we have a deal. The My Kid Could Do That gallery. Midnight, tonight. And tell her that I see what she does, and what she plans. Any harm comes to the woman or the girl, I will not share the secret."

"So what's the plan?"

"You'll figure it out. I can't hold your hand."

Laura's image fades. Her cup sits empty on the counter. Mom's painting is back in place, the frame still scorched. My powerful ally is gone.

You'll figure it out. What the hell? My primary earthbound asset, of course, is George. She doesn't answer. I leave a message. I try Rebecca. She picks up on the first ring. "Are you okay?" she asks.

Her concern is touching, but there is bad news to pass along. "I heard from Madam Augusta. I need to talk to you."

"I'm at the gallery. I'm scared, Vince."

"Stay there, keep the door locked. I'll be down in a few minutes."

❧

Twelfth Street is filled with revelers in strange costumes, spillover from the Wiccan street fair two blocks away. Fairies and nymphs. A new-age Mardi Gras. A white Escalade with smoked windows sits at the curb outside my building. My favorite mob hitter, Johnnie Tomasso, steps out wearing a shiny gray suit with a purple tie. I can't resist. "Tony Soprano called. He wants his car back."

He ignores my jab. "Tell me about Madam Augusta."

"Cops are looking for her."

"You think I don't know that?"

"I forgot, you have *contacts* in the Ninth Precinct."

"Forget that shit. Madam Augusta's gang shot three of my people last night, ripped off some valuable merchandise. We found them and evened the score. This is war."

"What's that got to do with me?"

"The cops raided an apartment in the East Village a couple nights ago. A bird tells me an old friend of yours was involved. I figure you must have some inside info."

"I haven't been a cop for a long time. They don't tell me what's going on." Partly true. Johnnie is standing with his back to the shiny, white Escalade. I stare at the side panels and the red paint sprayed across them: Ride The

Mole Train. The phantom graffiti artist has struck again. I can't hold back a smile.

"What's so fuckin' funny?" Johnnie spins around, following my gaze. Shock registers on his face. He runs toward the car, touches the still-wet paint, looks unbelieving at the smear on his finger, awed by the audacity of the insult. He has the car waxed every other day. He once broke a man's arm for brushing against the fender. To Johnnie, this is a cataclysmic insult.

He pounds on the car's roof. "Artie, you fuckin' asleep?" Johnnie's driver climbs out looking up and down the street wide-eyed. He wears a chauffeur's cap, a white sport coat buttoned over a hard-muscle gut. There's a gun in his massive right hand. Twelfth Street is packed with walkers and bike riders who show only casual interest in the spray-painted car as they push their way through the nymphs and fairies.

Artie shrugs. "I didn't see nobody, Mr. Tomasso." His gangster grammar takes him closer to the truth than he knows. Nobody did it.

A time that is not a time, a place that is not a place.

This might be the opening I've been looking for. I boom out a hearty, theatrical laugh. "Madam Augusta is messing with you, Johnnie."

He's back in my face, finger poking my chest. "Nobody messes with me, Vinnie-boy."

Macho Johnnie, swept along by his gigantic ego, might be an unwitting asset. "What are you doing tonight at midnight?" I ask him.

I tell him that Madam Augusta might be putting in an appearance at the My Kid Could Do That gallery around that time. It's a desperate measure that could put my wife and daughter in the middle of a firefight, but I don't see how I have any choice.

He likes the idea. "I'll be there." He stomps back to the Escalade, and with a final glance at his defaced ride, jumps inside. Artie peels out, probably heading for the paint shop.

It's almost eleven. An hour before I'm scheduled to call Madam Augusta and tell her the good news, that she's headed for the Mole Train. I won't mention the one-way nature of the trip. I hurry toward the gallery, where Rebecca is waiting.

⚜

St. Mark's Place is blocked off, lined with tents and tables vending all kinds of Wiccan shit. There's barely room to move on the sidewalk. The crime scene tape around the gallery is gone. I push my way through the mob clogging the sidewalks and the street, sporting butterfly wings, wearing tiaras. Rebecca opens the door and stares at me.

"What?"

"Your aura," she whispers. "You've seen—something."

"Let me in. I'll give you the whole story."

Two Wiccans I recognize from our meeting at the Enchantress wander around the gallery looking at the giant cakes and pies, but I sense they're barely seeing them. The rest of the coven, Rebecca explains, is working the Enchantress booth at the Wiccan Fair.

We gather in the office. Rebecca's phone rings, she goes into the gallery to answer it. She comes back and says, "Bridgett is going to be fine. She's out of surgery and we can bring her home tomorrow." The Wiccans respond with a smattering of applause. I'm going to throw water on the celebration. I stand behind Bridgett's desk and hold up my hand for attention.

"Madam Augusta called me this morning. She has my wife and daughter." Gasps, murmurs of sympathy.

Rebecca says, "What does she want to give them back? Although I think I know."

"Right. She wants access to the Mole Train."

"So what do we do?"

"To answer that, I have to tell you what happened last night in Tompkins Square Park, although I'm not sure myself." I tell them how Madam Augusta freaked out, turned and ran, how I thought I shot her son, how a flash of light and the roaring sound of a train suddenly exploded around me.

"Is that what scared Madam Augusta?" Rebecca whispers.

"This is where it gets a little weird," I say. "I never looked behind me in the park, but I know who was there, because she came to visit me in my apartment this morning."

Rebecca whispers in reverential tones, "Laura."

I tell them the whole story and they're an audience of true believers. "Laura saved your life in the park," Rebecca says.

I nod. "She wants me to tell Madam Augusta we'll make a trade: Jennifer and Becky for the keys to the Mole Train."

"Does it even *have* keys?" the blonde woman says.

One of the Wiccans, the thin blonde I recognize from the Enchantress, says, "Is the Mole Train even a thing?"

"Way above my pay grade."

"If we try to trick Madam Augusta, won't she—I hate to say this—retaliate against Jennifer and Becky?" Rebecca asks. "Jennifer is one of us. Shouldn't we have a say in this?"

"I'm open to suggestions."

The three stare back at me, silent. I let the silence hang, then I say, "Fine, I won't ask you to trust me, but trust Laura. She's knows things we don't even know there are things to know, if that makes any sense."

It's noon, my deadline for getting back to Madam Augusta, I motion everyone to silence and make the call.

Madam Augusta answers with no preliminaries. "Have you decided to save you family's life?"

"Laura Whitcomb saved your son's life. She has great power. She has agreed to give you the incantations for the Mole Train. Bring my wife and my daughter to the My Kid Could Do That gallery at midnight tonight. I'll be waiting outside. Laura has agreed to use her power to get you connected to the train."

"You will not trick me. Powerful spirits protect my soul."

"I value my wife and daughter's life. I know you have power over me." Rubbing it on a little thick, perhaps.

"You remember that. And you will be there?"

"Standing right out on the sidewalk," I say.

"Just you."

She's showing her cards there. She wants me dead. "When my family and I are safe, Laura Whitcomb will reveal the incantation."

We reach an agreement neither of us is likely planning to keep. Laura is the wild card. I have no idea how she plans to lure Madam Augusta onto a one-way trip on the Mole Train.

A minute after I hang up, my phone rings. George says, "Were you just talking to Madam Augusta?"

"I was. How did you know that?"

"We're the police. The tech guys have a tap on that phone."

A glimmer of hope. "So you have her position."

"Well, there's a problem. I'm standing here with the SWAT team, getting ready to blast her out of the underground trolley station, but it turns out she's out in Flatbush. Bronx PD moved in on her house, but they're saying there's nobody home. So where is she?"

"Don't know."

"What were you talking to her about?"

The critical question. I can't keep lying to George and hope to stay out of jail. "Not on the phone. Let's meet at Ginger's." I hang up before she can reply, run out the door toward Ginger's, ignoring the phone chirping in my pocket.

George slides into my booth at Ginger's. "I don't have a lot of time. I don't know if you heard, but there's a gang war going down on the Lower East Side. The Baca and the mob are mixing it up. We've had six killings overnight." I imagine the casualties of endless urban combat laid out before me. I hope it's not dream fodder.

"I've heard." I tell her of my meeting with Johnnie Tomasso. "I guess you know you have a spy in the precinct?"

She says, "I'm working on that. But one crisis at a time. Let's start with Madam Augusta."

"Madam Augusta has my family, she wants access to The Mole Train."

"Which doesn't exist," George says with a lift of her eyebrow. "You're getting reality and fantasy confused."

"I'll be the first to admit that, but reality is where the pain lies. And I'm feeling it. Jennifer and Becky could get killed in the middle of all of this. Please, I need your help."

George's expression softens. "First, you have to tell me what the hell is going on. What were you talking to Madam Augusta about?"

"We're going to make an exchange, tonight at midnight."

"Your family for an imaginary train? How does that work?"

"I've got some help in the imaginary department."

"And you also have a giant invisible rabbit?"

"There's another thing. I told Johnnie Tomasso that he might find Madam Augusta at the My Kid Could Do That gallery tonight."

"So your idea of keeping your family safe is to drop them into the middle of a gang war?"

"I had to do something. I didn't tell you, because that would put even more guns on the street."

"Funny, but 'protect and serve' doesn't usually translate into 'more guns on the street.' You gone all liberal on me, Vincent?"

"I've gone all 'keep my family alive.'"

"I understand, but my job is to protect *all* the people in the Ninth Precinct."

We argue tactics for a while, we finally agree George will put some undercover people around the gallery and try to make a quick grab on Madam Augusta, and maybe roll up a few of Johnnie Tomasso's guys at the same time. A SWAT team will be stationed out of sight a couple of blocks away.

"I'll explain the situation to the SWAT commander, but you have to realize things don't always work out perfectly in these situations. It's also possible that Madam Augusta's gang and the mob will shoot each other. We might not be able to prevent that." She stops short of winking, but her message is clear.

"One more thing, George. I need to borrow a bullet-proof vest."

Chapter Fourteen

The Ford van's dull green paint blends with the shadows under the trees in Greenwood cemetery. The perfect undercover vehicle, necessary now that the Mob has started a war. Three of Madam Augusta's gang are dead. But there is a little good news. She's had an influx of soldiers from a variety of Caribbean countries. Now, counting her two sons, her total forces number almost twenty. She has no illusions about them following the dictates of voodoo, but they are dedicated to the idea of making money.

She pulls out a long, bone-handled knife and slaughters another little albino alligator. Blood splatters her robe. She drains the carcass into the grass at the base of the tree, tucks her knife away, closes her eyes and gives herself over to the haunting sound of drums and flutes. A dozen of her followers sit in a circle around her in the darkness exchanging questioning glances. Madam Augusta chants as she dances, building to an emotional frenzy. One dreadlocked warrior, sitting cross-legged on the grass, smirks at the weirdness of her performance. He's rewarded by a withering glance from Little Jay

Madam Augusta releases a primal howl as the spirits take possession of her mind and body. Her heart races with joy. She collapses onto the grass, dripping with sweat. Her sons carry her to the van, off to the East Village to fight the battle of her life.

—❧—

My best protection is a crowd of witnesses. It's small comfort, though, to know they'll be able identify whoever shot me dead on the sidewalk. At a quarter to midnight, I step out onto the street in front of the My Kid Could Do That gallery. I leave the door open, per Laura's instructions.

Rebecca and the rest of the Wiccans are down the street at the Enchantress booth. Out of the line of fire. The Wiccan street fair is still going strong. A drum circle has formed nearby. Dancers and musicians weave their way up and down the street singing happy-sounding music. A joyful pagan celebration. Somehow, I'm not in the mood.

Nobody pays me any attention in my baggy, cover-your-bulletproof-vest shirt and cargo pants. Just some guy looking at his phone. So far, Madam Augusta's weapon of choice has been ergot powder. Bulletproof vest won't protect me from that.

I scan the crowd moving around me on St. Mark's Place. No sign of Madam Augusta, no sign of Johnnie

Tomasso's hoods. They could all be disguised as fairies and nymphs, but that's a stretch. I keep a lookout for Jennifer and Becky. Madam Augusta may have them doped up, or dosed with ergot.

My attention is drawn to a figure in a long purple robe moving toward me in a slow, drifty walk, face concealed by a hood. I'm suspicious of anybody concealing their face. A bummer, since half the crowd are wearing masks. The figure in the purple robe stands motionless, head bowed, hands lifted in prayer. She throws me a glance. Laura Whitcomb looks good in purple.

The action on the street is getting wilder, noisier. The music is growing; somebody has set up a PA system and people are crowded around a microphone, singing and playing weird-looking instruments. People dance in and out of the booths, arms linked in a joyous procession.

An old Ford van parks behind the barricade at the end of the block. Nobody gets out. I keep my eye on it.

Midnight plus five minutes. No sign of my family. I start to worry. Maybe this was a crazy idea. I watch the crowd, feeling more scared every minute.

Movement in front of me. A muscle-bound figure in dreadlocks and a tank top is moving toward me. He looks familiar. As he raises a pistol I realize he's the guy in the security video, the guy who carried Bridgett away. Before he can fire, a satyr dressed in buckskin steps up behind him and presses a silenced twenty-two to the base of his skull. The 'chuffing' sound is lost in the noise of the crowd. Tank top drops to the pavement, the satyr disappears into the crowd.

My phone rings and I glance at it. You don't take phone calls when you're under fire. My screen shows a flashing white display: Ride the Mole Train!

***

Madam Augusta moves slowly along St. Mark's Place, hips swaying to music only she can hear. Gede, the spirit of sex and death, inhabits her body, his power surges through her. Augusta smiles to herself, throwing her shawl over her shoulder in a gesture of defiance. She is fearless, more than a match for the witch. She is a hundred feet away from the My Kid Could Do That gallery, and there, just as ordered, is the ex-cop, Vince Richards, staring at his phone. It will be his last act on this earth. Her soldiers are hidden in the crowd. Laura Whitcomb is nowhere in sight.

***

I switch off my phone. This is getting ridiculous. A sea of smiling faces fills the street in front of me. Then, suddenly, four not-smiling faces. Madam Augusta's two sons push their way toward me. Little Jay is dragging Jennifer along. Wilky Mouton hobbles along on his broken foot, his arm around Becky's neck. My daughter is crying.

Rage blinds me and I reach for the Beretta in my waistband—and freeze. I can't fire into the crowd. Little Jay, however, has no such reservation. He yanks a gun out of his pocket. A sledgehammer blow to my chest throws me back against the gallery window and I slide to the ground. The sound of the blast brings a hush to the crowd. Or maybe my ears have stopped working.

A flurry of bullets fly around me, shattering the gallery windows, showering me with broken glass. A roar rises from the crowd. I wonder what they're cheering about, then the world fades to black.

Richards, the bastard cop, is down. Madam Augusta edges forward, shoulders pressed against the gallery wall. He's lying in a field of broken glass. Smoke trails from the muzzle of Little Jay's gun. She allows herself a brief smile, nods congratulations to her son, then steps up to Vince's body, slams her boot into his head. Vince Richard's family days—all his days—are over. The score is even.

He calls to his mother from the street. He and his brother are surrounded by the crowd. The Wiccans assault them with wooden swords and magic wands. The crowd cheers them on. Madam Augusta ignores his cries. Her sons can certainly defend themselves against a pack of elves and fairies.

She shakes her head with disgust as she watches the Wiccans pull Jennifer and Becky free from her son's grasp.

Her weakling sons have failed once again, but there is no time to worry about that now. Vince Richards is dead. What happens to his family is of no consequence. Madam Augusta turns her attention to the portal lying ahead. She can feel its pull. A figure in a purple robe steps into the gallery and motions for her to follow.

The gallery is awash in shadow. The yellowish glow of the streetlights throws distorted images of giant cakes and pies against the walls. Madam Augusta shakes her head. So this is what passes for art these days. She picks her way through the sculptures and moves down the back hallway. Laura Whitcomb stands beside a massive oak door bound with iron straps. She steps inside and motions for Madam Augusta to follow.

Though it might be a trap, the pull of the portal is strong and she creeps forward, inhaling the powerful essence of her spirit protectors. Energy courses through her, driving her into the darkness. Following the Wiccan Priestess.

Chapter Fifteen

"Come on, Vince. Wake up."

Rebecca's voice pierces the fog in my head, my vision blurs at first, then I focus on her face. Her brow is furrowed, there's a trickle of blood running down her cheek. The butterfly wings on her shoulders are crumpled, off at an angle.

"You been street fighting again?"

"Jennifer and Becky are okay."

Relief floods over me. The world spins, drumming and flute music fills my head. The Wiccan festival is still going strong. People stroll up and down the street. No interest in a guy lying on the sidewalk. This is the East Village

"Where are they?"

"They're fine."

"I want to see them."

"This is a little awkward. They don't want to see you."

"What do you mean they don't want to see me?"

She lays her hand on my cheek. "Are you okay?"

"My ribs feel broken and I have a hell of a headache. Where are they?"

She helps me up. "We're taking them to the hospital. They'll be okay. Becky is still pretty freaked out from seeing you. She doesn't want to talk about it."

My pain fades, overcome by a deep sadness. Whatever is wrong, there's no way for me to fix it. And, worse than that, I brought everything on myself. I never should have got Jennifer and Becky into this mess. All I can do now is find Madam Augusta and finish her. I know revenge is not the answer, but my rational mind is not in control at the moment.

Rage is building in me, I'm literally seeing red. I struggle to my feet. My vest caught Little Jay's bullet, but I can't account for the swelling behind my left ear. My hand comes away sticky with blood.

"Madam Augusta kicked you in the head. We ought to have that looked at."

"Later. Where is she?"

"Laura lead her into the gallery."

The thought that Laura Whitcomb might be in trouble brings me to my feet. Maybe there really is a Mole Train. I remember she told me I would see it when I believed it. I think I've finally become a believer. Maybe it's because I want it—need it—to be true. Madam Augusta deserves a one-way ticket to hell.

"Rebecca, call nine-one-one. Ask for Lieutenant Georgia Flores. Tell her I need backup."

"Where are you going?"

"Tell her I'm going to ride the Mole Train."

She shouts questions, but her words are lost behind me. I creep forward, holding a tactical flashlight alongside the Beretta. I slip through the maze of cakes and pies and into the office. The storeroom just beyond is filled with empty boxes, piles of frames and easels. The iron-banded door hangs open, the one that wasn't there before.

Stairs lead down into darkness. As I work my way down, the noise of the city fades. Then the roar of a subway echoes—overhead. That noise disappears and I descend into silence. The stairs end in a dark tunnel with a point of light at the end. I stumble along, fighting the dizziness in my head. In my weakened state, I miss the sound of footsteps behind me until it's almost too late.

A white flash lights up the blackness of the tunnel, followed by the echoing boom of gunshot. Chips of cement cut my cheek. I throw myself against the wall, toss my flashlight across the tunnel. My shooter takes the bait. A boom and the flashlight disintegrates. I moan like I'm hit. That generates a laugh from the shooter. Footsteps thump toward me. There are two of them. One of them drags a cast he is wearing from the foot I broke. Madam Augusta's sons. I hold the Beretta two-handed in front of me.

The footsteps stop. The shooter racks his slide. Dumb move. I fire at the sound. Three rounds as fast as I can pull the trigger. A scream and the gun clatters onto the floor. One down. Breathe, I remind myself. Breathe. My chest still aches from where he shot me. We're even. Son number two creeps forward, dragging his broken foot along. I track his progress with the Beretta. "Give it up, kid."

He ignores my shout and rushes me. I can't shoot an unarmed kid with a broken foot, no matter how much I might want to. I remember the powder he threw in my face the first time we met. He's not exactly unarmed.

I retreat along the tunnel, keeping my gun on him. The point of light at the end is growing brighter. The light shows me his faint outline. Sure enough, he has one gloved hand extended as he pegs along. He puckers up to blow the stuff in my face. I tuck and roll, bring my foot up into a sweeping kick sending him down on his back. He raises his hand for another try with the powder. I grab his hand, fold it back on him, dumping the powder in his face. But somehow, he's back on his feet, fingers clutching at my throat. I work the Beretta up between us and shoot him in the heart.

I check Little Jay. His sightless eyes stare at the ceiling. A pool of blood is forming around his head. The light at the end of the tunnel silhouettes a running figure, robe billowing around her legs, hair bound up in a turban. Madam Augusta. I run after her.

❧

Madam Augusta feels her pulse race as she steps onto the platform. At last, her goal is in sight. Vine-covered walls made of pale yellow stone open onto a vast, starry field, receding to infinity. The silence of a tomb shrouds the space.

A feeling of excitement grows in Madam Augusta's chest. Voodoo spirits are all around her in this place. Beads of sweat form on her forehead and the feelings overcome her. She begins to dance, swaying to music unheard—faster and faster until her breath comes in gasps. She stops, hands braced on her knees, realizing the platform is empty.

Laura Whitcomb had deceived her. Madam Augusta screams out to her spirit guides. The silence mocks her. Rage boils up in her chest. She clenches her fists and spins around looking for her deceiver. There, just stepping onto the platform, is Vince Richards, the man responsible for all her troubles. She reaches in her pocket for the leather bag of ergot.

❧

I step into the light and realize I'm entering a subway station like the one the Uber driver lured me into. The walls are shiny, the color of the lemon cake in the gallery. Vines cover the walls. Figures in period costumes, frozen in place, dot the platform. The tunnel is a smooth tube, no rails. Madam Augusta stands at the edge of the platform staring at me, rage in her eyes.

Behind her is an infinity of stars, the kind of thing they always call awe-inspiring. It scares the shit out of me. A flash of light catches my eye. Madam Augusta turns to face the sparkling abyss, drawn as I am to a speck of light in the distance racing toward us like a shooting star.

A team of skeletal horses appear out of the star field, black leather harness bounces on their boney shoulders as they gallop past us. Then their bones float apart and reform themselves into a ghostly outline of an old steam locomotive with massive driving wheels and a funnel smokestack. The train now travels on ribbons of bone-white rails. An engineer in a flowing white robe sits at the throttle. His dead eyes, set deep in a Greek profile, stare straight ahead. A rush of air hits me and I stumble backward.

Usually, only poets and mystics manage to peek behind the veil into the dark side that runs like a river beneath us all. Even rarer is the person who has experienced the dark power that seeks to control our lives, firing up the engine of our basest nature. And the unlikeliest thing of all is that such a person would be a private eye from the East Village. A force has flowed across the ages from the annals of Greek mythology to the subways under the East Village. It has been called many things from the time of the Greeks. It once inspired the Salem witch trials. Now, it has come to be called The Mole Train.

The locomotive is followed by a procession of passenger cars, images blurred by the speed of their passage. At the speed the train is traveling I lose count of the cars and then, gradually, the train slows and I see car after car, all brightly lit, crowded with passengers, all staring straight ahead. The wheels have become the claws of monstrous crabs. The train slows, then jerks to a stop, centering a single car on the platform.

It's painted a glistening maroon with gold trim, and bears the logo, "The Central Massachusetts Railroad," a train that went out of business a hundred years ago. It's ablaze with light. Full of people. The women passengers wear bonnets and high collars, the men, top hats. I count twenty-three passengers, travelers from another century, sitting silently, staring straight ahead. I remember the twenty-three people hanged in Salem two hundred years ago.

A door slides open and Laura Whitcomb steps onto the platform. She wears a gray linen frock. Her auburn hair is pulled into a bun.

She says, "Blessed be, Madam Augusta."

Madam Augusta steps back, crosses herself. Her turban hangs askew, her dress is soaked with sweat. "Where is the real train?"

"This is the only train and it won't be here long."

"Tell me what it is I must say," Madam Augusta says.

"There are no words to controls its power. Not for one who seeks to do evil. This is a train for the good, a sanctuary for the dead."

"The spirits protect me, give me power. This train will give me more."

"This train will destroy what you have become."

"You are lying, trying to keep me from my rightful due."

"You have many enemies on Earth who wish you harm. Here, no one cares if you die. There is a difference."

I have the Beretta trained on Madam Augusta's back. I edge toward her, tell her, "This is as far as you go." Madam Augusta spins around, throws a handful of ergot powder at me. I step back—almost make it out of range.

The train shudders into motion, sparks spin off the wheels, become a kaleidoscope of whirling discs and flashing lights. A sonorous voice in my ear: *"This is a time that is not a time, this is a place that is not a place."*

I shrug off the hallucination, shake my head, draw in deep breaths, pull myself up onto my knees and watch helpless as Madam Augusta rushes toward Laura, hurls the powder at her, bag and all. It settles over Laura's head, giving her a ghostly visage, but her expression doesn't change. Her voice is calm. "Leave this place. There is nothing for you here."

"No. I will not leave. The spirits protect me."

"You're in pain. The only way out of the labyrinth of suffering is to forgive." Laura steps back on the train. It starts to move, gains speed. Madam Augusta jumps on after her, clutching at her dress.

I grab a handhold two cars down and throw myself onboard.

Chapter Sixteen

I advance along the aisle in an awkward, stumbling jog. My eyes still burn from the ergot powder. I hang onto the seats, trying to ignore the silent passengers sitting motionless, staring straight ahead. The eerie thing about my train ride is the utter silence. The cars are brightly lit but the view out the window is a montage of shadows. Apparently, time and space have gone out the window.

I spot Madam Augusta ahead of me. She turns and pulls out a nasty-looking knife. Hatred contorts her face, her eyes are angry slits. She growls in her throat. Understandable. I've killed most of her family. The heat of her fury drives me back. She holds the knife low, waving the tip in slow circles, showing me she knows how to use it.

She slashes at my gut. I block it, throw a punch at her head. I'm rewarded with a slice across my arm. It burns like hell. I try a front kick, forgetting that you never kick above the waist, except in karate tournaments. She grabs my heel and upends me in the corridor. By the time I stumble to my feet she retreats out onto the open landing between cars.

I follow. The light from the cars spills out onto the landing, revealing a blurry ladder of cross ties racing beneath us. We circle each other in the silent, windless space. My eye is on the knife. My bulletproof vest won't stop it. She comes at me again. I grab her wrist. She is surprisingly strong and she twists out of my grip, slashes at my face. I bat her hand away, barely in time. She is kicking my ass. I pull up the Beretta.

A varnished mahogany door in the next car opens and Laura steps out. "That's enough."

I lower the gun. Madam Augusta cries, "Bitch, you lied to me."

Laura shakes her head, points at the door behind her. "Here is what you're looking for."

Madam Augusta grabs the brass knob and eases the door open, suspicious of a trick. The car is decorated with elaborate carvings and statuary. It's bathed in a faint glow from purple stained-glass windows. Seats upholstered in red velvet line the car. The passengers stare straight ahead. A few unfreeze themselves, turn their gaze on Madam Augusta. Seated up front are Little Jay and Wilky Mouton, the two sons I just killed back in the tunnel. A tall, handsome man who I take to be Haitian, and a white-haired man beside him smile up at Madam Augusta. Her husband and her father, the men I killed on the Lower East Side a decade ago. Madam Augusta throws down her knife and starts to cry. Her son ushers her to the empty seat beside him. The whistle screams, an oddly musical note. Augusta sits down and lets out a long breath. A smile spreads across her face.

I remember what Laura wrote in her Book of Shadows: Love is the fire that turns the earth. The thing that powers this train. I had been thinking, a *one-way trip straight to Hell*. The Mole Train is headed in the other direction.

Laura guides me out onto the landing. We're slowing down.

"This is where you get off," she says.

"We were just getting acquainted."

"Goodbye, Vince." She puts her hand in the middle of my back and, with surprising force, throws me off into the blackness.

I'm too surprised to brace myself. Whatever I've landed on is hard. I suffer a crack on the head, black out for a moment. When I come to, I recognize the station I just left, the vine-covered platform, the frozen folks in their period clothes. The train slows to a crawl. Its sad, bluesy whistle echoes off the yellow walls.

A little ways down the line, outlined in the train's amber headlamp, sits a shiny black Audi, stalled half-way across the track. The driver throws open his door and jumps clear just as the cowcatcher slams into his car, sending a torrent of twisted metal floating into the blackness. The driver, bald head shining with sweat, dances with rage beside the tracks.

The train picks up speed, recedes to a bright dot and disappears. I raise my hand but I'm waving at an empty star field. The sound of claws clattering on stone segues into the moan of a distant train whistle. Is there a lonelier sound? I wonder what car Hank Williams is riding in.

My Uber driver, eyes flashing with anger, turns to me and, in a surprisingly earth-bound gesture, gives me the finger.

Then he is gone and I lie in total darkness.

Chapter Seventeen

Not sure whether I dozed off or passed out. Sometimes there's a fine line between them. I wake up to the sound of a familiar voice: "He's back here. Get those fucking paramedics." George in command. Strong hands lift me onto a gurney. We're rolling into the My Kid Could Do That gallery. George walks alongside, cradling my head in her hand.

A paramedic unfastens my bulletproof vest, looks me over. "I thought you got shot." She sounds disappointed. No lifesaving for her to do. She busies herself checking my vital signs. I realize that though I've been shot and stabbed, I never felt better. The soreness in my chest is gone. The gash Madam Augusta put in my arm has healed into a faint pink line.

George helps me off the gurney. "You missed all the excitement, Vincent."

"What excitement?"

"Not much, just a little gang war. The Baca gang and Johnnie Tomasso's boys got into a running gun battle through the East Village. A dozen bystanders got killed, but in the end the two gangs managed to pretty much wipe each other out. SWAT rounded up the survivors. Still the lead story on CNN."

"And when did this happen?"

She gives me a strange look. "Just after midnight. I couldn't find you anywhere. I came back in just now to take another look around and all of a sudden, there you were, stretched out in the hall. So everybody's accounted for, except Madam Augusta and her two sons."

"I don't think you'll have to worry about them anymore."

"Do you know something I don't know?"

"Where are Jennifer and Becky?"

"Rebecca told me they're safe and doing fine. Wouldn't say where they were. That part of the drama is not police business. I hope you guys work things out."

Not police business. My business. "And the Wiccans?"

"Some of them got a little bruised up, but they're doing fine. I don't think they're street fighters."

"They might surprise you."

"While you were gone, the spectacle of a gang war at a Wiccan street fair caught the whole country's fancy. The My Kid Could Do That gallery went viral. Calls started coming in. Rebecca told me there was a bidding war. All her plastic pies and cakes sold out."

"Eco-friendly representational acrylic renderings."

"Whatever. She grossed almost a million bucks."

"Too bad your kid didn't do that," I say.

"I don't have a kid."

"Not sure I do, either."

"That's sad."

That plops our conversation into an awkward silence. George excuses herself, walks away talking on her phone. Yellow crime scene tape stretches across the front of the gallery, covering the shattered windows. All Rebecca's pie and cake sculptures carry a little red 'sold' dot. My mother's painting is back on the gallery wall.

As soon as George is gone, Laura's image reappears in the scorched picture frame. She looks at me with a wistful, what-might-have-been expression. Or at least that's how I imagine it. I smile at her. Her image fades. My mother's painting fills the frame.

I listen for a train whistle, but hear only the sound of early-morning East Village traffic. Things are almost back to normal. One more loose end. I call Rebecca.

"I'm sorry about Jennifer and Becky," she says. "They made me promise …"

"I know. Not your fault. One question. When Becky looked at me in the hospital, she screamed like she'd seen the devil himself. What did she see?"

"I talked to her a few minutes this morning, just before they left. She said your face looked *exactly like hers*, same ponytail and everything. She freaked out."

"I can see why."

"She said she loves you."

I don't trust my voice at this moment. I mumble a thank you and hang up.

George walks up. "You look like you *haven't* seen a ghost."

I smile at her surprising insight. Maybe she knows something I don't know.

"I'm off duty," she says. "Want to get some coffee?" She tucks her phone back in her pocket.

"Are you ever gonna tell me about it?"

"Here's my plan. It's almost dawn, you're off duty. I say we go back to my place, crack open the Johnnie Walker Green and have a heart-to-heart. Who knows what we might uncover."

"Sounds provocative."

"You have a problem with provocative?"

She throws a playful punch at my shoulder. We laugh, walk toward her cruiser.

We end up in the darkness of the underground parking garage next to my apartment. I slide next to her. She closes her eyes, tips her head back. She is still one of the great kissers of all time.

After we come up for air, she says. "You insulted my plant. It's not a service thistle, it's a guard thistle." Spiky fronds snake over the dash, creep up the windshield.

"Sure it is."

George pulls me toward her until I'm lying across her on the front seat, feeling her warmth. We struggle out of our clothes. A sharp pain in my backside. I look over my shoulder. The thistle hovers over my nether regions. There's a sparkle in George's eyes, but I don't think it's love. That train has left the station.

About the Author

John is the author of eight novels and numerous shorter non-fiction works. He has conducted writing workshops, classes and seminars around the country for the past 20 years; his sensitive and insightful critiques have inspired hundreds of writers. His classes on the novel, short stories, essays and magazine writing have given many students a stepping stone to publication. Currently, John is editing a book-length collection of essays by Northwest writers.

johnreedbooks.com

The Original
DUNGEON SOLITAIRE
Tomb of Four Kings

Still Available for Free

at

matthewlowes.com/games

Complete Rules
are Print-Ready and Playable
with any Standard Deck
of Playing Cards

Complete Rulebook
&
Labyrinth of Souls Tarot Deck
Available at
matthewlowes.com/games

Labyrinth of Souls Fiction
Ten books available now!

coming soon

The Ruptured Firmament by Stephen T. Vessels
Aftermath by Cynthia Coate-Ray

For more information, visit

shadowspinnerspress.com

www.ingramcontent.com/pod-product-compliance
Lightning Source LLC
Chambersburg PA
CBHW021658110726
47902CB00007B/1975